Halfway to You

A WEST TINDALE ROMANCE

ELLE WHITTAKER

LEMONADE
HEART
PRESS

ISBN (print): 979-8-9909996-0-2

ISBN (e-book): 979-8-9909996-1-9

First Published 2022, Second Edition Published 2024, Third Edition Published 2025

Cover Design by Ink & Laurel

Content Guide

This book contains:

Adult language/profanity, people confidently owning their desire, and consensual open-door sex scenes

Parent death (past)

Contents

West Tindale, Montana
HALFWAY TO YOU
To footpaths
To Tindale National Park
SILVERVIEW WAY
The Old Schoolhouse
(Shops)
Little Park Theatre
Merrel's Grocery Store
Dottie's Candy Shoppe
West Tindale Visitor's Center
Hitching Post Hotel
Jerry's Fly Fishing shop
The Bar
ALLEYWAY
PINE RIDGE AVE
City Park
Bonino's Italian Restaurant
Winslow Books
Dairy Queen
Zhaos' Lucky Dragon
Real Estate Office
(Shops, incl the knife shop)
West Tindale Adventure Co
OLDVIEW WAY
(Shops)
5TH AVE
West Tindale School Field
West Tindale School
(Shops)
Happy Bear Restaurant
Clinic
Post Office
Happy Bear Hotel
4TH AVE
(Homes)
Richland's Auto Repair
7 Eleven
Happy Home Trailer Park
Smith's Hardware Store
Movie Theatre
3RD AVE
CVS
Library
Rental cabins
(Apartments)
Holiday Inn
Ruby's Restaurant
Hungry Wolf Pancake House
(Homes)
GRIZZLY WAY
TINDALE WAY
OUTPOST WAY
2ND AVE
Little Tindale Inn
KOA
Church in the Pines
(Homes)
Bonino's old house
1ST AVE
American Horseback Adventures
West Tindale City Offices
(Homes)
West Tindale cemetery
To Silver Falls

Tindale National Park

HALFWAY TO YOU

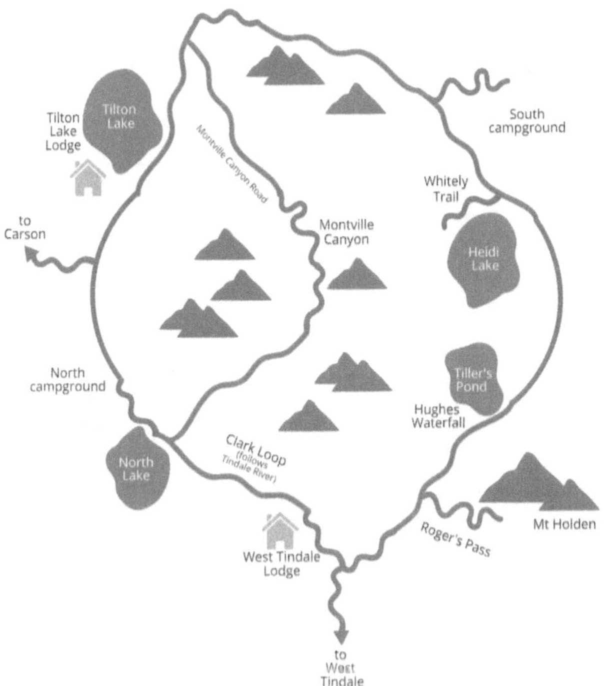

NOTE ABOUT INDIGENOUS HISTORY

Tindale National Park is a fictional place, based loosely on Yellowstone National Park in Wyoming and Montana. Indigenous peoples lived in that area for centuries before Europeans explored and named specific locations. Yellowstone was home to the Newe Sogobia (Eastern Shoshone), Cayuse, Umatilla, Walla Walla, Apsàalooke (Crow), and Tsètho'e (Cheyenne) peoples.

If Tindale National Park were a real place, it would likely share a similar history of colonization. The names of mountains, lakes, and other features would be the result of European occupation.

Out of respect for indigenous peoples, I did not wish to create an artificial Native American history for Tindale National Park to acknowledge. But I also did not want the history of colonization in this country to go unacknowledged.

I encourage readers to research the indigenous peoples who lived and continue to live in the places you call home.

For all the hopeless romantics

"Aggressive platonic cuddling." That's what Anne always called it. She was sitting with Roberto Bonino on the couch, the whole house to themselves, the basement illuminated by just the flickering TV screen. The Bonino family had just moved into this house a few months ago, and no one could get over how much room there was. Anne was tucked into Roberto's arms, her head on his chest, like they'd sat so many times before. When you've grown up with someone your entire life, it seems natural to touch. She and Roberto were used to holding hands, draping their legs over each other's laps while doing homework. They weren't dating. It was just affection.

Like tonight. Anne startled when there was a jump scare, even though she'd seen this episode of the X-Files a dozen times. Roberto laughed and held her tightly. "Platonic comfort" from her best friend.

But somehow tonight it felt…less platonic. Tonight, Anne was suddenly aware of how Roberto's skin felt, the warmth of him beneath her.

Roberto loosened his arms around Anne, but then,

hesitantly, he moved his thumb in slow strokes up and down her shoulder and arm…so slowly, every movement a question mark, singing through her. When the episode ended, neither of them moved. Anne didn't know how long they sat like that, Roberto's thumb brushing against her arm, her head on his chest, both of them aware of the other's breathing.

They both jumped when Roberto's cell phone went off. Anne lifted herself up and reached over Roberto to hit "ignore," then looked up at him. She could feel the air crackling between them.

It started to become too much. They were on the edge of something and Anne couldn't find her footing. So she stood and held out her hand. "Come on!" she said.

"Where are we going?"

"Moonlight cemetery ramble!"

Roberto grinned and took Anne's hand. "My favorite summer tradition," he said. They'd graduated high school a month earlier, and only had so many summer nights in West Tindale before they headed off to college in New York together. Anne and Roberto walked the one block to the cemetery, holding hands as usual, the moon so bright it cast shadows. They wandered between the gravestones until Anne collapsed onto her back, gazing up at the stars.

Roberto lay next to her, his shoulder touching hers.

"I can't believe we get to live here," Anne said softly. "The stars are so bright."

Roberto turned and looked at Anne. She turned to him with a small smile, and then looked back at the sky again. "I like living in a place where the stars are so bright. Like, the moon is almost too bright."

Roberto smiled and sat up, then turned and placed his hands on either of Anne's head, blocking the light. "Is this better?" he said.

"Much better, thank you," she laughed.

"Good. I don't want you to go blind from the moon."

Roberto smiled down at Anne, laying beneath him, her hair spread out around her head. Their laughter slowly died out as they looked at one another.

Roberto's eyes moved from Anne's lips to her eyes to her lips again, and then he leaned forward and gently pressed his lips to hers.

The kiss flooded through Anne, and she kissed him back, reaching up and placing a hand on his chest. This wasn't a "spin the bottle at a dumb teenage party" kiss or a weird theatre club stage kiss. It was an "I want to kiss you" kiss. It was a "this could be more" kiss.

Anne pulled Roberto towards her, but his cell phone rang again. He rolled over and pulled it out of his pocket, grumbling good-naturedly.

But then he frowned at the screen.

It was the last night Anne ever saw him.

CHAPTER 1

Family Dinner

ANNE

"Well, that was a bigger turnout than we expected," Anne said, bringing the last folding chairs to the back room. Her red curls were coming free from her braid, and she'd long ago thrown her cardigan off. Her mom, Debbie, glanced up from the computer at her desk in the office, which was actually just a converted storage closet.

"Things *were* pretty crowded out there," Debbie replied, then looked back at the computer screen and sighed. Debbie's own curly hair had gone gray years ago, but she still dressed like the hippie she was—all peasant skirts and crystal pendants.

Anne finished leaning the chairs against their place in the back room, a large handwritten label with the word "chairs" taped to the wall behind them. She walked over to the office and leaned against the door frame. "How did we do today?"

Debbie sighed. "We've done worse, but we've also definitely done better. Your father would be horrified at these spreadsheets if he was alive." Debbie took her reading glasses off and turned to Anne. "I don't know why people don't buy books anymore."

"Mom, it's October. The bookstore is always slow this time of year."

"I know."

"And I've got some ideas for the holidays. I'll show you my bookstore planner tomorrow."

Debbie sighed again. "Thank you. I just…things were different when you were little, and it just felt like we weren't hustling so hard. I don't know if this is what you had in mind to do with your life. Trying to save the family bookstore."

Anne smiled. "Working here is part two of The Plan. I already did part one and went to college in New York City, and now I'm here helping my mom run the family bookstore. We'll worry about saving it when it's actually in danger."

"What about part three?" Debbie asked.

"What about it?"

"Marry a nice boy and settle down in West Tindale?"

Anne waved her mother off. "Eh, I'll worry about that later."

The bell at the front of the bookstore rang. Anne called over her shoulder. "Sorry, we're closed!"

"It's me!" a voice called out.

"Come on back, Cosimo!" Debbie replied.

Cosimo Bonino walked into the back room, two plastic bags in his hands. "I brought leftovers," he said, setting the bags down on the table in the middle of the room. His gray hoodie hung off his shoulders, and he was still wearing his apron from work. Debbie stood up and hugged the young man. He was on the shorter side, but Debbie was tiny, so she still had to reach up.

"Thank you, sweet boy," she said. "Slow night?"

Cosimo nodded. "It's getting…difficult. If I'm being honest, I don't know how much longer I can sustain it."

Debbie reached out and rubbed his arm. "I know what you mean," she said. "We were just talking about the same thing when it comes to the bookstore."

Anne watched Cosimo and her mother for a moment. It was hard to listen to the people she cared about worry. But if Anne had learned anything in the past few years of her life, it was that problems were a lot easier to solve when you weren't hungry. She started opening the bags. "Pollo alla parmigiana?" said hopefully.

"Not unless you can learn how to pronounce it," Cosimo said as he re-pulled his long hair into a ponytail. Anne smiled at him while Debbie brought plates and silverware over. The back room had served as a kind of second kitchen for as long as Anne could remember—so long that they had "downstairs dishes" and "upstairs dishes."

"What would we do without you?" Anne said as she loaded up her plate.

"Starve," Cosimo replied.

"That might actually be true," Anne said.

"Anne, why don't you marry Cosimo?" Debbie said.

"Mom, Cosimo is gay," Anne replied, taking a bite of chicken.

"But think how well you would eat for the rest of your life," Debbie sighed. "And it would be so convenient! The restaurant is right next door, you could live there and still help at the bookstore."

Cosimo spoke. "I mean, I would marry Annie if she'd have me, but it would really be more of a roommate situation."

Anne reached over the table and laid her hand over

Cosimo's. "Thank you, Cos," she said, with mock sincerity. Cosimo clasped her hand back.

"As deeply touching as that proposal is," Anne continued, "If you want grandkids, Mom, I'll have to go with someone other than Cosimo."

"Good thing Cosimo has a brother," Debbie said, with a wink.

There was an awkward pause.

"Yeah, that's not going to happen," Anne replied.

"Why not?" Debbie said.

"Because Roberto Bonino lives in Chicago and does not want to leave Chicago and also I haven't spoken to him in almost a decade."

Debbie turned to Cosimo. "How's Robbie doing nowadays?"

Cosimo shrugged. "Good, as far as I know. We don't talk much."

The table went silent for a moment. "Well," Debbie finally said, "I know your mom and dad would be very proud of both of you boys. I wish they could see how well you've done."

Cosimo smiled. "Thanks, Debbie," he said, then turned to Anne. "And if you want to marry Roberto, I'd be fine with that."

Anne rolled her eyes.

AFTER DINNER, Anne sat in her attic bedroom and opened her bullet journal. She'd chosen a "locks and keys" theme for the month of April, with turn-of-the-century flourishes. She pulled out her pens. Her journal may have seemed like a lot of work to other people, but keeping track of things relaxed her. The art of it relaxed her. Coloring things in, doodling, seeing it all laid out. It was proof that life could be orderly. That you could make plans and keep them in place. She flipped to the day's spread and checked off the to-do list items she'd accomplished. (Read for 30 minutes, check. Pay credit card bill, check. Poetry Night prep, check.) She colored in the small bottle she had drawn to track how much water she drank.

Her pen hovered under the banner "Highlight of the Day." She smiled and then wrote, "4-year-old Emily Young reciting her poem about trees at Poetry Night, followed by thunderous applause."

She was halfway through her to do list for tomorrow when her phone dinged. A message from Maya.

> MAYA: Trucker date was TERRIBLE. Going home to my vibrator. I hate men.

Anne smiled, then typed out her reply.

> ANNE: If you hate men, why do you keep dating them?

> MAYA: Because I ran out of women in West Tindale.

Anne smiled again, then responded.

> ANNE: I'm sorry your date was terrible.

A few minutes later, a voice memo popped up. Anne hit play.

"This fucker tried to convince me that we should get a room at my PARENTS' HOTEL because it was quote-unquote free, which it would not have been, and he didn't want to go back to his place because it turns out that he literally did not have a place. Like, I don't know if he was trying to get laid or just get a hotel room. Probably both. I kept trying to make it clear that I did not want to go to any place with him and that if he was going to get a hotel room he was going to pay for it with money."

Anne typed out:

> ANNE: Didn't you fuck that one hot construction guy in a free room at your parent's hotel once?

Maya replied:

> MAYA: Yes, but I wanted to fuck that one hot construction guy so that's why the room was free.

Anne laughed.

> ANNE: Tell me more about it at lunch Wednesday?

> MAYA: Yeah, go finish your bullet journal for the night.

Anne laughed again.

> ANNE: You know me so well.

Anne put her phone down and finished her to-do list for the next day (groceries, brainstorm Christmas bookstore event, finish watching documentary). She paused again as she got to the last section of the page. "On my mind." She thought back to dinner with Cosimo and mom, how Debbie had suggested she marry Roberto. She hadn't thought about him in a while, but every now and then, someone or something opened the gate in her mind and he came strolling in. She sighed and then wrote, "Roberto Bonino."

She fell asleep hugging her pillow.

CHAPTER 2

Get Your Shit Together

ROBERTO

Roberto Bonino grabbed the shot glass from in front of him and threw it back. He wasn't sure how many drinks he'd had, and the lights of the club were flashing erratically in the dark room, so he also couldn't tell if his vision was a little blurry because of the lights or the alcohol.

"Hey, you didn't wait for me!" the girl next to him shouted, trying to be heard over the music. He couldn't quite remember her name. Sheema…? Shiva…?

"I'll get another one!" he shouted back. When the bartender set another shot in front of Roberto, he and the girl clinked their glasses and threw them back. He turned the glass upside down on the bar and glanced at the girl. *She's pretty*, he thought. He liked the way her spine led up to the soft wisps of hair that she had swirled into some kind of twist.

He reached up and ran a hand through his own hair, so dark brown it was almost black. It was the same color as the stubble along his square jaw, the five o'clock shadow that would appear a few hours after shaving no matter what he did.

Roberto's phone buzzed. He pulled it out and saw a text from his brother.

COSIMO: Hey, do you have a minute?

Roberto swiped the message clear and glanced at the time. 3:17 a.m. What the fuck was Cosimo texting him at this hour for? He had already left a message earlier that day, asking to talk. Which was why Roberto was in this club now. Because he really didn't want to talk with his brother, especially if the conversation started with something like "Can we talk?" Those words never meant anything good.

So he'd decided to drown them in alcohol and sex.

The texts and voicemail would make more sense if he and Cosimo texted or talked regularly at all. But theirs was generally a "holidays and birthdays" kind of relationship. He imagined that whatever Cosimo had to say could probably wait. With both of their parents gone, and having never known their grandparents, they didn't have any other family. But Roberto had spent years telling himself he was fine with that, until he eventually believed it. It was easier to live his life without having to worry about parents or siblings or a wife or kids.

For example, if he had a wife and kids, he wouldn't get to be at this club tonight, with this gorgeous woman. This is why he loved living in Chicago. He didn't have to answer to anyone. If he wanted to go out and have a good time, he could.

"Come on!" The girl grabbed Roberto's arm and led him to the dance floor. She turned around and ground against his body, and Roberto loosened his tie and hugged her spine to him. His phone buzzed in his other hand. Cosimo again. Roberto hit "ignore" and put the phone in his pocket, then pressed his hips against the girl's body. It felt good, to feel her there. He was disappointed when she pulled away. She wriggled her body to the music, and for a moment he couldn't figure out what she was doing. Then he felt her press something into his hand. He looked down to see a scrap of black lace fabric and realized it was the girl's underwear.

She smiled at him and walked towards the bathroom. Roberto grinned and followed her through the crowd.

HE WOKE up to his phone ringing. He groaned as he squinted at the screen. Cosimo. What the hell could possibly be so important? Roberto rolled over, then looked around blearily. He was in his own bed, alone, although he wasn't completely sure how he'd gotten there. He couldn't remember much of the night before, after he and the girl had snuck back out of the bathroom.

He glanced at his phone again. 8:13 a.m. He also had a text from Lily.

> LILY: Hey, work wife here. Where the hell are the updated plans, asshole?

Roberto groaned again. They had a presentation to a new client at nine that morning. He texted Lily back.

> ROBERTO: On my way to the office. I'll email you plans in a minute.

Roberto sat up, his head pounding. He looked over at the aspirin and full glass of water on his nightstand. Drunk Roberto (or whoever had gotten him home, he still couldn't quite remember) had clearly tried to take care of him, but he had definitely not done his part.

He reached over and took the aspirin, drinking the full glass of water, and peeled off his sweat-drenched clothes from yesterday. His shower was miserable, but by the time he got into his Uber, he was feeling at least functional. He emailed the updated plans to Lily, then checked his voicemail. One message from Cosimo. Roberto hit play.

"Hey, Roberto, it's Cosimo. I know it was late when I called last night, so sorry about that. But I have a possible job for you, so if you could give me a call back, that'd be great." There was a brief pause. "Miss you. Okay, bye."

Roberto sighed and leaned his head against the cool glass of the car. He couldn't imagine any job that Cosimo had for him that would be better than the work he had in Chicago, and he really didn't feel like talking to his brother. *After the presentation,* he thought to himself. *I'll call him after the presentation.*

BUT HE DIDN'T GET a chance to call Cosimo after the presentation, because after the presentation, his boss called him into his office.

"Have a seat, Roberto," Julio said. Roberto tried not to collapse into the chair.

"I'm sorry," Roberto said as he sat down.

Julio folded his hands on his desk and looked at them for a long moment. When he looked up, his eyes were full of concern. "Roberto," he said, "I'm going to be as honest as I can be. That was the worst presentation I have ever seen in the history of this company."

Roberto grimaced.

"First of all," Julio continued. "You look like hell.

Second of all, you stumbled through the whole thing, did not know answers to basic questions from the client, and at one point, I was worried you were going to throw up. I'm being as direct as possible with you because I want you to understand how unacceptable this is."

"I know," Roberto said, hanging his head in his hands. "I know, and I'm so sorry."

Julio leaned back and sighed. "Are you drunk?" he asked.

Roberto slowly shook his head.

"Are you hung over?"

Roberto paused, then nodded.

Julio leaned forward and put his hands on his desk, then looked up at Roberto. "Okay," Julio said. "Normally I'd give people some benefit of the doubt, but we may lose this client because of today. I'm taking you off the project."

Roberto's head snapped up. "Permanently?"

"Permanently. I'm also taking you off the charity projects committee. I'm moving you to assist on the Markville Offices."

"But the Markville Offices are…that project doesn't start for another four months."

"That's right."

Roberto looked at his boss. "So in the meantime…?"

"In the meantime, I'm telling you to take an unpaid leave of absence."

The office was silent for a moment, as Julio's words landed.

"Am I fired?" Roberto asked.

Julio shook his head. "No. But this isn't the first time something like this has happened with you."

Roberto started to say something to defend himself, but Julio held up a finger to stop him. "You've been with us for two years, and you're a good architect. But I think you need to take some time to figure out if this is what you want to do. I think an unpaid leave is the best way for you to do that." Julio paused. "Speaking as a friend, and not your boss…get your shit together, Bonino."

Roberto nodded, then stood. "Thank you, sir. Anything else?"

"That's all."

When Roberto left, Lily was waiting for him in the hallway. She fell into step with him as he walked back to his office, her chestnut brown hair falling over her shoulders.

"How did it go?" Lily whispered.

"Well, I'm not *technically* fired," he replied.

"Technically?"

"I have been given a four-month unpaid leave of absence, though, so."

Lily stopped in her tracks. "Oh shit," she said, then started walking again.

"'Oh shit' is right," Roberto said. He pushed the door of his office open and sat down. Lily leaned against the doorway when Roberto added, "He also told me that I need to quote-unquote, get my shit together."

Lily didn't say anything. Roberto looked up at her. She studied his face for a moment and said, "I mean…"

"What the hell, Lily."

"I'm just saying! Maybe Julio is right!"

Roberto wasn't sure what to say to that, so he didn't say anything at all.

"Are you gonna be okay?" Lily finally asked. "Like, financially?"

Roberto stared at the floor for a moment. "I have enough to pay bills for the next four months, but not much more."

"What about savings?" Lily asked. Roberto gave her a look.

"Oh my god, Roberto. Where the fuck does your money even GO?"

Roberto shrugged. "Art? Alcohol? Door Dash?" Lily shook her head. "I'm pretty sure Julio will take me back on after this. If not, I'll find something else."

"What are you gonna do?" she asked.

Roberto sighed. "Call my brother," he said.

CHAPTER 3

Pages and Pasta

ANNE

It was late by the time Anne got home from her day in Silver Falls. The bookstore had closed an hour earlier, so she unlocked the door and let it swing closed behind her as she set down half of her bags. She knew her mom was probably in the back room, going through sales from the day. "They were out of receipt paper," she called out. "A two-hour drive to Silver Falls for them to be out of receipt paper. But I got more pens and—"

Anne halted. Her mother and Cosimo were sitting in two chairs at one of the small tables in the bookstore, each holding a glass of champagne. They cheered when they saw Anne.

"Annie! Come have champagne!" Debbie said. Cosimo stood and poured a glass.

Anne was still frozen. "What's going on?" she said.

"Una celebrazione!" Cosimo replied, handing Anne a glass.

She set the other bags down, then looked at the wall that normally separated the bookstore from Cosimo's restaurant next door. Shelves had been haphazardly shoved out of the way. "And the uh…" Anne began. She couldn't quite make sense of what she was seeing. "And the gaping hole in the wall behind you?"

Debbie smiled. "We're merging!"

"Merging?" Anne asked.

"The bookstore and the restaurant," Cosimo said. "We're opening a bookstore café!"

"If we knock down the wall between our two places…" Debbie began.

"Then we can combine the businesses," Cosimo finished.

"And we want your artistic eye, Annie," Debbie added. "You've got to help us plan. We need a new layout, new branding, new signage—"

Anne studied the hole in the wall. It was about the size of her fist, and she could see through it to Cosimo's restaurant next door. "We need an architect," she said.

"I have an architect," Cosimo replied.

"We need money," Anne added. "How are we funding this?"

Debbie waved her hand dismissively. "I got a loan."

"For how much?!"

"I'll show you the books later. Oooh, because you'll need to know your budget anyway. But isn't it exciting? How lucky are we that Bonino's Family Restaurant shares a wall? Drink your champagne, Anne!"

Anne tipped her glass back without thinking, then sat down in another empty chair.

"A bookstore café, huh?" she finally said.

"We're still coming up with a name," Cosimo said as he sat back down again. "'Winslow Books and Bonino's Family Restaurant' is too long."

Anne thought for a moment. "Books and…Bruschetta."

"Yes, something like *that!*" Debbie replied. Anne could tell her mother was a little tipsy.

"Books Bolognese," Cosimo said.

"Books and Biscotti," Debbie added, giggling.

"How did this start?" Anne asked.

"You said 'Books and Bruschetta,'" Debbie replied.

"No, the entire thing. The merger idea."

Cosimo nodded. "Last night after I came over to bring dinner to you guys, and you went to bed, Debbie and I started talking about finances. We realized that some months, the restaurant does better than the bookstore, and other months it's the other way around. I made some joke about how much easier our lives would be if we could share the profits, and then your mom had the idea to join forces. And today she knocked a hole in the wall to make sure it would work."

"Mom just knocked a hole in the wall?"

Debbie reached out and patted Anne's hand. "With a hammer," she said, smiling.

"And then Debbie went to the bank and got a loan and now we're merging."

Anne sipped her champagne and glanced at the hole in the wall. "And if it doesn't…work?" she asked.

Debbie shrugged. "Then we both go out of business."

Twenty-four hours later, Anne was trying to explain the plan to her best friend over appetizers at the bar. "She just shrugged?" Maya asked, biting into a mozzarella stick. "She just shrugged and said 'Then we'll both go out of business'?"

"She was so cavalier about it!" Anne replied. "And the whole thing was so sudden…like, she had the idea and then immediately went to the bank and then knocked a hole in the wall."

"It's her wall," Maya said. She reached up and ran a hand through her long brown hair, revealing glimpses of piercings up and down one ear.

"Technically, it's the bank's wall," Anne replied.

"Well, soon it will be no wall."

Anne leaned her head on her hand, elbow resting on the bar. "True. We just have to do a whole bunch of construction and re-decorating and re-branding and paperwork in like, six months before the summer season starts next year."

Maya mirrored Anne's pose, head resting on her hand. "I'll do a spell to help you. Six months is plenty of time, assuming you all know anything at all about construction."

"We definitely do not," Anne replied. "But Cosimo said something about having an architect, so I'm just crossing my fingers that whoever it is will keep everyone and everything on track."

"Well, your mom and dad knew what they were doing when they started Winslow Books all those years ago. Debbie probably knows what she's doing now. And Cosimo's been running that restaurant basically single-handedly for like eight years."

Anne nodded. "I'm still going to be very anxious about it for the next few months, if that's all right."

Maya grinned. "I can't stop you. You're a Virgo through and through." She grabbed another mozzarella stick. "Are you sure you're not just upset because The Plan was to help your mom run a bookstore and not a bookstore café? This fucks everything up."

Anne laid her head on her arms. "Oh god, I hadn't even thought of that," she said.

"Relax, my little control freak. I'm sure it will be fine."

Anne lifted her head again. "This is too stressful. Distract me. Tell me about that trucker date."

Maya rolled her eyes and sipped her beer. "Thank the good goddess Gaia that dude was just passing through. I finally just told him point-blank that I wasn't interested in anything more and that I was going home. Literally left him in the parking lot."

"Feminists everywhere are proud of you for being direct."

"I swear, you give a guy one hand job in a movie theatre and he thinks you're inviting him back to your place."

"You…gave him a hand job in the movie theatre?!"

"Eh, kind of. Not like, to completion," Maya shrugged. "I just felt him up a little."

"Completion," Anne repeated.

"Yeah, I hated that as soon as I said it," Maya laughed. "What about you? Given any hand jobs in movie theatre lately?"

"First of all, no," Anne said. "Second of all, that actually sounds kind of fun. But I'm pretty sure I'll have to find my true love somewhere else and then convince him to move to West Tindale, where everything is dead and snowed in for half the year, and then crawling with tourists to the adjacent national park for the other half of the year. Because clearly, my Prince Charming is not in West Tindale. Or Silver Falls."

"You could marry my brother."

"Ew. Not that I don't love Devan. But it would kind of feel like marrying my own brother?"

Maya laughed again. "Fair enough," she said. She raised her glass. "To true love, wherever it may be," she said.

Anne clinked her glass. "Wherever it may be."

CHAPTER 4

What Do You Want?

ROBERTO

After his disastrous presentation and his meeting with his boss, and talking through things with Lily, Roberto shut the door to his office and laid his head on his desk. He was still hungover and still did not want to talk to his brother. It took Roberto a solid ten minutes to work up the strength to dial the number. He knew he'd never do it if he didn't do it today. Cosimo answered on the third ring.

"Hey," he said.

"Hey," Roberto replied. "You called?"

"Yeah. Is this a good time?"

Roberto glanced around his office. "Good a time as any," he said.

"I've got a proposal for you," Cosimo said. "I know you've got work and stuff in Chicago, but if you could take a two-week break, I've got a job for you here at home."

"What kind of job?"

"The Winslows and I are combining the bookstore and restaurant into one big bookstore café, and we need an architect to help with the renovation."

Roberto had the vague sensation of the earth shifting

very subtly beneath him. He had somehow assumed that everything in his hometown would remain exactly the same. Then again, he had also assumed that he'd have a job in Chicago for the next few months, but that was not happening.

"I might have some time," Roberto said. "I'd crash with you, right?"

"Yep," Cosimo replied. "And it's a paid gig. It's not a ton of money—definitely not what you're making now, I'm sure, but it would be a huge favor, and it feels right to keep it in the family."

"Right." Roberto was silent. Cosimo waited.

"So, do you want to do it?"

"Let me think about it for a day or so. You can text me details." Roberto already knew he had the time, and could definitely use whatever measly sum Cosimo could pay, but the idea of returning to West Tindale for a few weeks, especially to help with the Winslows was…a lot.

"Sure," Cosimo said. "Just let me know in a few days."

A few moments later, Lily knocked on Roberto's door again.

"Hey," she said. "I came to grab the hard copies of the Dooley plans."

"My career isn't even cold in the grave and you come in here, asking for blueprints."

"Stop being a baby. It's not your whole career." Lily sat in the chair on the other side of Roberto's desk and crossed her legs. "What did your brother want?"

"They're renovating the restaurant and they want to hire me to help."

"Well, that's something productive to do with your time

off," Lily said. Roberto made a non-committal noise. Lily leaned back and swung one leg, her high heel dangling from one toe. "Are you going to do it?"

"I don't know," Roberto said. "I don't know if I want to."

"Well, can you get your shit together in West Cowboyville, Montana, or are you going to just sit around on your ass in Chicago?"

"Honestly, the sitting around on my ass sounds okay at this point." Roberto stood and reached into his filing cabinet.

"Right, but do you actually want to do that?" Lily paused, and looked at Roberto.

"I don't…know?"

Lily stood up and took the blueprints from Roberto. "Well, I'd like an answer by E.O.D. today," she said, smiling. "Send your response by email."

Lily walked out of Roberto's office and shut the door behind her.

It was vaguely annoying that two people in his life had told him that he needed to get his shit together, in the same day. His life was fine, thank you very much.

Although he *had* just completely fucked up a major presentation because he was too hungover, and he had a vague memory of some kind of sexual encounter with a girl whose name he couldn't remember in a club bathroom the night before, and he wasn't sure if they'd used a condom. And he'd kind of just lost his job, at least temporarily. He had very little savings. And if he was honest, he didn't really have many friends, aside from his boss and Lily and her husband Kai.

What DO I actually want to do? Roberto thought.

A handful of answers popped up in his mind. *I want to*

have a good career. I want to not feel like I'm crawling out of my skin. I want to not fuck up my life.

No one ever thinks their life is out of control. *What's that they say in AA?* he thought. *"Admit that your life has become unmanageable."* Well, as far as he could tell, his life was still manageable. If you didn't count the epic failure of a presentation earlier today. Or the girl in the club, or the money thing. Roberto leaned back in his chair and stared at the ceiling.

If he was completely honest with himself, his instinct was to go out again tonight, to get fucked up and not have to think about his massive failure at the presentation that morning. That should probably be a red flag. Maybe Lily and Julio were right.

What do you want, Roberto Bonino?

Roberto took a deep breath. "I…want to get my shit together," he said quietly. Almost like he was trying the phrase on. He paused and tried to envision what that would look like. It would probably not look like getting completely shit-faced on weeknights. And as fun as it was to fuck strangers in club bathrooms, he thought he might want to try actually going on a real date now and then. He knew everyone involved in those one-night stands was a grownup, himself included, but still. And he should definitely pay more attention to using protection.

He didn't imagine a complete one-eighty in his life. Having his shit together would look like going out for drinks now and then, learning peoples' names. The occasional barbecue or dinner with Lily and Kai. Working on buildings he cared about. So more like a thirty-degree turn. Maybe forty-five.

He didn't like the idea of spending two weeks in his tiny Montana hometown, but he wasn't sure if he could keep his head on straight if he stayed in Chicago. In West Tindale, there weren't as many places that he could fuck himself up. Roberto rubbed his face. This wasn't exactly rock bottom, but he could admit that things weren't exactly going well.

He ran his hand through his hair, pulled his phone out and texted Cosimo.

> ROBERTO: I can help with the renovation. If I text you flight info, can you pick me up from the Silver Falls airport?

CHAPTER 5

West Tindale

ANNE

Anne grabbed a stack of flyers from the counter of the bookstore. "I'll be back in a few!" she said to Debbie, then she stepped outside into the bright October air. In a few months, there would be so much snow that it would be difficult to get around town without a snowmobile. For now, Anne could still walk to deliver flyers, so she turned and strode down the street. She had a walking loop that she made around town every month, distributing updated flyers for events at the bookstore.

Anne had lived in West Tindale, Montana, for almost her entire life. The town was almost exactly one square mile—about a mile from the north end to the south end, and a mile from the east end to the west end. The bookstore was about two blocks from the east side of town, right up against Tindale National Park.

During the four years that Anne had lived in New York, she'd missed having Tindale Park right outside her front door. Even when she spent time in Central Park, she was aware of the city pulsing just outside of its edges, throwing light and sound up into the sky above. Nights in

29

Tindale were so dark that you could see the Milky Way year-round, and there were some summer nights when the moon was so bright that it cast a shadow, and you could walk along the roads in West Tindale without a flashlight.

Anne pushed open the door of the fly-fishing shop across the street.

"Hi Jamie!" Anne called out.

"Hey, Annie!" a low, gravelly voice replied from around the corner. It was the same voice that Anne had been hearing when she walked into this shop for as long as she could remember. She reached up on the bulletin board by the door and pulled down last month's flyer, replacing it with this month's.

"Tell your mama I said hello," the voice said. Anne knew Jamie was sitting in a rocking chair behind the counter, flipping through a magazine or watching a baseball game on the tiny TV, like he always was.

"Will do!" Anne replied.

She had similar exchanges at Dottie's Candy Shoppe, at the knife shop, and at the West Tindale Visitor's Center. She said hello to Tyler and Corinne at the Adventure Company. The summer tourist season had mostly ended, and except for a few brave visiting souls, the town would remain quiet until the coming May. A handful of shops completely closed up during the off-season. The one thousand or so full-time residents of West Tindale didn't have any need for t-shirts, postcards, or other souvenirs, so those shop owners spent the winter down in Silver Falls.

Anne's last stop was always Zhao's Lucky Dragon, the Chinese restaurant two blocks away from the bookstore. Anne sat down for a few minutes to chat with the owner, Joe. A few years ago, he'd tried to teach her how to pronounce his Chinese name, and Anne thought she was getting better at it, but Joe had just laughed the last time she attempted to greet him with it.

Now he smiled at her as she opened the door. "Hello, Annie. Are you hungry?" he said.

Joe had moved to West Tindale when he was in his thirties, almost three decades earlier. Anne had been fed steadily by the Bonino Family and the Zhaos growing up, and even when she was in New York, she'd missed their cooking.

"If you have any pot stickers ready, I'll take a few," Anne replied.

"Of course," Joe said, walking down the hall. "How is your mother?" he called from the kitchen.

"Good!" Anne said. She decided to hold off on talking about the merger they were planning with the Bonino's Family Restaurant. "We're doing another drawing contest for the kids this coming month, if you want your grandkids to enter."

"I'll tell them," Joe said, bringing out a plate of pot stickers and sauce. He sat down across from Anne and handed her a pair of chopsticks.

"Is that Annie?" a voice called from the kitchen. Joe answered back in Mandarin. An older woman came around the corner. "Did you eat?"

Anne held up a pot sticker. "Joe is feeding me, Mrs. Zhao."

"Mom, sit down," Joe said. "Mark told you to stay off your foot for another week."

Mrs. Zhao waved her hand dismissively. "Eh, sons always worry."

"He said it as the clinic doctor, not as your son," Joe replied.

"I've got to go anyway," Annie said, standing up, stuffing one more pot sticker in her mouth. She leaned over and hugged Mrs. Zhao warmly, then did the same with Joe. "Thank you for the food."

Anne's heart swelled as she left Zhao's Lucky Dragon. The Zhaos, the Boninos, Jamie…they were like family. In a town as small as West Tindale, some people might feel stuck, but Anne had always felt at home.

And there was also the fact that most of these people had known her father, could tell her stories about him that she was too young to remember.

He'd died while on a fishing trip when she was five. Loyal Winslow had planned on going to Berry Dell Lake, but at the last minute, he'd changed plans and gone to the Otter River. No one could tell them exactly what had happened, but in the spring, the water was always higher, and his boat had flipped, trapping him.

Anne's memories of her father were hazy. A warm cotton shirt, a low voice rumbling a bedtime story with words she couldn't quite remember now. Laughing when his beard tickled her skin. He'd loved Tindale Park his entire life, and Anne had inherited his love of it. Growing up, she spent her summer days swimming and hiking in the park, and her summer nights playing Fugitive and Capture the Flag in town. It was the perfect town to play night games in—one square mile was exactly big enough to keep the game interesting, and small enough to keep it manage-able. (Although once, when they were fifteen, Devan swore he saw a wolf on Tindale Way, so they kept flashlights and bear spray with them after that.)

But she loved West Tindale. She knew when she was young that she wanted to stay here forever. And that hadn't changed. That was The Plan.

CHAPTER 6

Think of It Like Rehab

ROBERTO

A few days after being given his leave of absence, Roberto pulled his suitcase out of his walk-in closet. *West Tindale*, he thought to himself. There were so many things about West Tindale that he hadn't thought about for ages. The family restaurant that his brother now ran. The house they'd only lived in for a few months before that night when he was seventeen. But he didn't want to think about that house.

Roberto stood in his closet and gazed over his suits and business wear. He realized that they'd be out of place in West Tindale. He'd spent his entire childhood and teenage years wearing jeans and t-shirts and flannels, and when he had left, it had taken him a few years to shift his wardrobe. Standing in front of his closet now, he grabbed whatever casual clothes he had and put them in his suitcase.

His phone dinged to remind him that he had to head to the airport soon. He'd have to program the lights to the apartment to come on with a timer while he was gone. Not that he was worried. The apartment building was accessible only by key card, and you needed a code to even get through the gate. It was a far cry from the dingy studio he'd found for himself when he first moved to Chicago. At age seventeen, he'd gotten a job at a pizza place, and had worked there all through college. He'd lived in a handful of apartments, but moving into his sleek high-rise two years ago had been one of the proudest days of his life. He and Lily had drunk champagne until they were both sick, and fell asleep on the new couches in their clothes.

He'd have to remember to tell housekeeping not to come either, he thought. He glanced over at his hand weights. He couldn't remember if West Tindale had a gym, but he doubted it. He threw his running shoes into his bag. He'd gone on his fair share of business trips, and had gotten pretty good at packing.

Out of habit, Roberto pulled his nightstand drawer open and reached out to grab a handful of condoms. But halfway there, he stopped himself. Why would he need condoms in West Tindale? The entire town's population was roughly 1,000 people, most of whom he grew up with and would almost definitely not be having sex with. For a very brief second, Anne's face flitted through his mind, but he batted it away. The largest nearby city was Silver Falls, with its booming population of 50,000, and its two bars. Roberto sat on his bed.

He reminded himself of his thoughts on his last day of work. That maybe it would be good for him to take a break, anyway. It was only two weeks. He'd survive going that long without sex. It wouldn't be the end of the world. He closed his nightstand drawer.

After grabbing a few toiletries and his laptop, he zipped up his suitcase and pulled out his phone to get an Uber. Then he sat and looked around his apartment.

He remembered picking out furniture with Lily and Kai, arguing over "form versus function." (He'd decided to mix both equally.) He had bought paintings and prints to fill the walls—the kinds of things he'd wanted for years but couldn't afford until he'd been hired at Jiménez Building Design. He and Lily had both been hired there at the same time.

Lily had lived in Chicago her whole life, and whenever Roberto thought about it, it felt so strange to him. For a while, he thought it was because the place where he'd grown up was so small, but that wasn't quite it. It was that the idea of staying in one place your whole life was strangely...undivided, like a book without any chapters.

Looking back on his life so far, Roberto could clearly divide his life into three separate chapters. Chapter One was growing up in West Tindale. He had spent his winters trudging to school through the snow, and his summers playing Capture the Flag. Chapter Two was moving to Chicago, young and alone and crazed with grief, spending years in tiny apartments, and eating ramen after six hours of classes and eight hours of work.

And now he was in Chapter Three. Working at an architecture firm, living in an apartment where you needed a code to get into the building, going to clubs and swiping through dating apps on weekends. The thought of returning to Chapter One now made him feel slightly claustrophobic. He pulled out his phone and texted Lily.

> ROBERTO: What if I don't actually want to get my shit together in Montana?

Lily replied right away.

> LILY: Tough shit. Think of it like rehab. You're taking a break in scenic Buttfuck, Montana.

Roberto sighed and his phone dinged again. His Uber

was here. He picked up his suitcase and walked downstairs. Another text from Lily came in.

> LILY: Just be in the room. Whatever room you're in, be in it.

Roberto closed his eyes for a moment. It was the advice he and Lily had taken turns giving each other for years. Roberto just didn't think he'd ever be in a West Tindale room again.

Anne's face came to mind again. Or at least Anne's face as he remembered it. He didn't use social media, so his most recent memories of Anne were from when they were both seventeen, just out of high school. He wasn't even sure if she was still in West Tindale. If she was, it was inevitable that they'd run into each other. Especially given the project he was going to work on.

Roberto's stomach twisted as he got closer to the airport. Maybe this was a bad idea. He knew spending two weeks with his brother would be tough for its own reasons, but he'd also be working with Debbie, and possibly Anne. He thought of the last time they'd seen each other, and then decided that he did not want to think about the last time they'd seen each other. It was just for two weeks. He could survive two weeks.

A Revised List

ANNE

Anne reached up to brush her hair out of her eyes as she pushed a box aside with her other arm. She and Maya were in the upstairs storage room, pulling out boxes of holiday decorations for the bookstore downstairs.

"Oh my god!" Maya yelled. "Look at this!"

"Maya, focus on the task at hand," Anne said. This was the fourth time Maya had been sidetracked by some discovery.

"But it's Baby Anne's 'Ideal Man List'!" Maya yelled. "I can't believe you framed this."

Anne stopped what she was doing and looked over. "Oh my god," she said.

"Making lists even back then," Maya replied. Her eyes glanced over the eight-by-ten framed document as Anne walked over. "How old were you when you made this?"

"Knowing me, there's probably a date on it…yeah, there. I was…ten?"

"Ten-year-old Anne knew what she wanted."

Anne looked over Maya's shoulder and then laughed.

"'One, knows how to waltz,'" she read aloud. "Very

important skill for a lasting relationship. 'Two, plays guitar.' Also foundational for marriage."

"Do you think you'd be willing to budge on number five?" Maya asked. "It's overly specific."

Anne took the document from Maya's hands and scanned it. "'Five, drives an orange Bronco.' Why…was that important to me?"

"Probably because Tyler Young's family had an orange Bronco."

"Oh my god, you're right!" Anne covered her face and laughed. "Oh, Tyler Young," she said. She kept reading. "Oooh, is five is overly specific, eight is the opposite. 'Handsome.' That's it."

"Still valid, though," Maya said. "I kind of wish I'd made one of these when I was young. I wanna see how it compares to what I want now."

"I imagine your 10-year-old list would have been pretty similar to mine."

"Informed by Hallmark movies and extremely hetero-normative?" Maya said, smiling.

"Same thing," Anne replied.

"True," Maya said.

"What would you have put on your list?"

Maya leaned against a stack of boxes. "'Handsome,'" she said. "Probably some dumb shit about having a pickup truck."

"We do live in West Tindale, after all," Anne replied.

"True. I probably would have had something gross like 'loves God' or 'honors his mother.'"

"I agree that the 'loves God' thing isn't great, but a guy honoring his mother is still nice."

"I'm into it if it's like an 'honor the divine feminine' thing and not a patronizing misogyny thing. Because goddess knows I also love the divine feminine."

Anne thought for a moment. "Do you think you knew you liked girls back then? When we were ten?"

Maya sighed. "I definitely liked girls back then, but I don't think I knew I liked girls back then. And honestly, you don't really think about it when you're ten…romance is just sort of an abstract, distant idea. So when I say I 'liked girls' I mean I just sort of hyper-focused on a girl and wanted to play with her at recess all the time. But in my head, I like 'I want to be best friends with her!'"

"Even though I was your best friend," Anne said.

"Right," Maya replied, then looked at Anne. "It's kind of weird that I never had a thing for you."

"I have spent my entire life feeling slighted."

"Yeah, sorry. The heart wants what it wants. Also, I found the holiday boxes."

"Oh good." Anne smiled, then set the framed paper aside.

In bed that night, Anne kept thinking about the list they'd found. Eventually, she got up and sat at her desk, then opened up her bullet journal.

She thought about the handful of dates she'd gone on in college, some better than others. Garrett swam up in her memory, the ways they got along so well, and the ways they didn't. It wasn't that Garrett wasn't a good man. It was just that after a while, she had the sense that he was walking a different path than she was—like their paths were diverging very, very slowly. When they were walking in the same direction, it was easy to hold his hand. But eventually, they were far enough apart that Anne had to choose between leaving her own path and letting go of Garrett's hand. So she chose to let go of his hand.

She already knew the shape of the life she wanted—a quiet, homey life in West Tindale. But perhaps her vision could have some clarity. It was like she had the outline, but not the color.

It took her almost an hour to do, but after lots of doodling and brainstorming, Anne had a new list. It was shorter than the one she'd made when she was ten, but it was truer now.

Anne's Ideal Man (A revised list made at age twenty-five)

1. Appreciation for the arts. Doesn't necessarily have to be an artist, but someone who can enjoy museums and concerts and poetry with me.

2. Enjoys "the comforts of home." A fan of sitting in front of the fireplace or enjoying a meal with family or sitting in the backyard and chatting.

3. Willing to communicate. It sounds all trite and basic, but someone who's willing to say what's on their mind and ask questions and not be afraid of feelings.

4. Kind. Wants good things for the people he cares about. Compassionate.

5. Handsome.

6. Likes kids, or is at least interested in parenthood.

Anne sat back. It really wasn't that long of a list. She didn't think she was being too specific, or that her standards were too high. The problem was that she couldn't think of anyone she knew that met her criteria. Or where she would have to go to meet this person.

And there was the conundrum.

She wanted a happily ever after, and she wanted it in West Tindale. But to get that happily ever after, she was pretty sure she'd have to leave West Tindale. She hoped she could convince whoever this person was to move back to her tiny hometown with her. But who knows, maybe someone right now was daydreaming about living in a cabin in a place like West Tindale.

She sighed, then closed her bullet journal and went back to bed.

CHAPTER 8

The Bonino Family Restaurant

ROBERTO

R oberto had spent two weeks away from work plenty of times. And he planned to do it again. In places like Cancun. Hawai'i, maybe. Places with margaritas and bare skin and above-freezing temperatures.

He had not ever envisioned spending two weeks in West Tindale.

When Cosimo picked him up from the airport in Silver Falls, they hugged awkwardly. Roberto realized it had probably been at least three years since they'd last seen each other in person—the Christmas that Cosimo came out to Chicago. Cosimo looked just a tiny bit older than he had then. A hint of gray in his long dark hair. Maybe his smile lines were a little bit deeper.

The two-hour drive to West Tindale was mostly silent. When they pulled into town, Roberto frowned at a building on the corner of Silverview Way and 1st Avenue. "Is that new?" he asked.

"Oh yeah, that hotel was built about a year after you moved away," Cosimo replied. "It's been doing pretty good. The owners are nice."

Roberto kept feeling jolted between the familiar and the unfamiliar as they drove through town. There was the 7-Eleven that he and Cosimo used to ride their bikes to. The school still had the same murals painted on the side. But the Nilsson Family Pharmacy had been replaced by a CVS. The playground at the park had new, different equipment. Roberto felt vaguely annoyed that the town had changed at all, which he knew was unreasonable, but he didn't like the idea of it moving on and growing.

"Hey, thanks again for coming out," Cosimo said. "I know it's not up to your usual pay grade, but it really helps us out."

"Sure," Roberto said absently, looking out the window. "I had the time off work anyway."

Roberto hadn't told his brother the details of why he had the time off work, but didn't think it was absolutely necessary to share.

"You'll have to take a look at the shared wall to make sure this is even possible," Cosimo said, "But Debbie and I were thinking of just taking that whole wall down and kind of just starting from scratch with a big open space."

Roberto was only half-listening. "Yeah, we can look at that."

"The two spaces are so different right now, just in terms of look, so once we land on a formal vision, we want to make sure the whole thing works together."

"Works together, got it." Roberto's phone buzzed. Lily.

> LILY: Hey, did you land safely? How's it going out in the Wild West?

Roberto tapped out a response.

> ROBERTO: Landed fine. Getting into West Tindale now. There are no good bars, no nightclubs, or anything else interesting. Just fucking trees.

Three dots, then Lily's reply:

> LILY: Quit whining, Bonino. You're there to get your shit together, and if anything's gonna help you do that, it's fucking trees.

> ROBERTO: I'm not going to fuck a tree.

> LILY: Ha ha. Get your shit together.

The car stopped and Roberto looked up from his phone.

He and Cosimo sat in the car for a few moments, both gazing out at Bonino's Family Restaurant. *At least this hasn't changed*, Roberto thought. Same orange and yellow lettering over plates of pizza and spaghetti and breadsticks. Same wooden benches out front. Hell, even the curtains in the apartment upstairs were the same white lace.

"Welcome home," Cosimo said.

"Yeah," Roberto replied. He stepped out of the car and grabbed his suitcase from the back.

When Cosimo opened the door and flipped the lights on, Roberto was temporarily frozen. He hadn't remembered that his family's restaurant had a smell…bread and floor cleaner and dust. For a second, he was a teenager again, a red apron tied around his waist, bringing orders back to the kitchen. Roberto shook his head and looked around.

Same red checkered plastic tablecloths and wooden chairs. Black and white photos of Naples and Venice and

Rome on the walls. Roberto noticed a set of new frames near the register. He set his suitcase down and walked over. In one frame was a picture of Roberto and Cosimo, sitting on either side of a woman in her forties, all of them holding popsicles and laughing. Zia Maria. Roberto hadn't thought about her in years. When Roberto was little, maybe eight or nine, the Boninos had hired Maria to help with the restaurant. She waited tables, did dishes, sometimes just made sure Roberto and Cosimo were entertained. The boys had worshipped her. Their parents, Tom and Gabby, had loved her because she grew up in Italy and they could talk about home with her, and Roberto and Cosimo had loved her because she snuck them cookies and told them stories and taught them how to sing old Italian songs.

In the other frame was a picture of his parents when they were young, maybe in their mid-twenties, standing in front of the restaurant. They were both laughing, arms around each other. The other frame held a typed-up page of a few paragraphs.

Bonino's Family Restaurant was established by Tommaso and Gabriella Bonino when they first arrived in West Tindale from Positano, Italy, a small town on the Amalfi Coast, shortly after they were married.

Tommaso Bonino was the son of a wealthy textile merchant, and Gabriella Moretti's family ran a small laundry. The two met on an afternoon when they were both seventeen. Tommaso brought textiles to Gabriella's family business, and it was love at first sight. They spent hours that first day talking and laughing, and soon discovered a shared passion: food. Both Tommaso and Gabriella loved cooking. He invited her to his family's house for dinner that night.

But while the dinner Tommaso cooked was delicious (and the tiramisu that Gabrielle brought was pronounced "perfect"), Tommaso's family made it clear that they disapproved of the match. As the oldest son, Tommaso was expected to take over the family business one day, and his parents thought Gabriella was beneath him.

So Tommaso and Gabriella did what any sane seventeen-year-olds would do in this situation—they eloped.

After being married secretly at a church in the next town over, the newlywed Boninos boarded a ship for America, and then a train bound for West Tindale. They were answering an ad calling for caretakers for the West Tindale Lodge.

Two years later, Tommaso and Gabriella started Bonino's Family Restaurant, serving authentic Italian food to the tourists who flock to Tindale National Park every summer. It eventually became a true family business, with their sons Cosimo and Roberto helping out. The restaurant became a staple of the West Tindale community.

Roughly two decades after they had established their family restaurant, Tommaso and Gabriella Bonino both died in a car accident while on their way back from Silver Falls in winter. Their two sons, ages nineteen and seventeen at the time, were not with them. Today, the restaurant is run by their oldest son Cosimo, who strives to keep their legacy alive through food and a sense of belonging. The Bonino family has always cherished how food can be a way of showing love, and they hope that you find love here today.

Cosimo came and stood next to Roberto.

"Annie wrote that a few years after you left," he said.

"Anne wrote this?" Roberto asked.

Cosimo nodded. "I couldn't think of how to say any of it."

Roberto felt something inside his chest tighten. He opened his mouth again. "Is she still—" But before he could finish, the door burst open.

"Roberto!" a voice called.

Roberto resisted the physical urge to scrunch his shoulders up around his ears. He knew he'd have to see old familiar faces sooner or later, he had just counted on it being later. He turned around and smiled.

"Hi, Mrs. Winslow."

"Mrs. Winslow?! What the hell is that?! It's Debbie. Come here and give me a hug, you idiot!"

Debbie grinned and held her arms open, and Roberto walked into them. She squeezed him tight, rocking from side to side. The tight thing in Roberto's chest filled with warmth. He realized that it had been ages—maybe even years—since he'd been hugged like this. He swallowed hard.

Debbie pulled away and held him at arm's length. "Well don't you look like a proper rebel," she smiled. "With your dark swooping hair and your piercing blue eyes and your motorcycle jacket." Roberto ducked his head in embarrassment.

"It's not a real motorcycle jacket," he said.

"Well, still," Debbie said. "Come have dinner! Annie just set the table next door, but we can set an extra place for you."

Roberto shook his head. "Thanks, Debbie, but I'm exhausted. I think I'm just gonna head up to bed."

"Your old room is ready for you," Cosimo said.

"Thanks," Roberto replied. "Good to see you, Debbie." And he walked upstairs.

It was true that Roberto was exhausted, but lying in his childhood bedroom, he had a hard time sleeping. He hadn't been in this room for eight years, and it made him feel seventeen again, which he didn't exactly enjoy. He shifted against the pillows. Some nights, he would lie in this bed, thinking about Anne, knowing her bed was right on the other side of this wall. Waiting to hear her soft knock to tell him good night. Roberto found himself smiling before he felt his chest tighten again.

"You're just here for a couple of weeks," he whispered to himself. "No need to revisit old…attachments. Just do the job and get back home."

He fell asleep clutching his pillow.

CHAPTER 9

The Architect

ANNE

At seven the next morning, Anne's alarm went off. She had the same routine every morning—she had a spread about it in her bullet journal and everything.

> 7 am: Wake up. Make the bed even if
>   you're in a hurry, because it only takes
>   thirty seconds and it makes your whole
>   day better.
> 7:10 am: Yoga.
> 7:30 am: Breakfast
> 8:00 am: Shower and get ready
> 9:00 am: Start the day (bookstore, errands,
>   etc.)

Her bedroom could technically fit her yoga mat, but most mornings she did yoga downstairs in the bookstore. The apartment upstairs was essentially just a kitchen, two bedrooms, and a bathroom. The bookstore downstairs functioned as their living room most of the time. But even besides that, Anne loved being among the shelves of books in the quiet of the early morning. In the summer, the light would come in around the curtains, and in winter, she would sometimes look out onto the snowy streets before stretching into the day.

Anne pulled her hair into a ponytail, threw on leggings and a tank top and sports bra, and walked downstairs to the bookstore with her yoga mat under her arm.

She was surprised to see the lights already on, and she jumped to discover a stranger measuring the wall with the hole in it.

A shirtless stranger.

At least she assumed he was a stranger. A stranger with back muscles for days.

Anne blinked. Whoever this guy was, his arms and shoulders were toned and strong, and his back was smooth and tight, and his sweats hung off his hips in a way that made Anne forget how to form sentences. One of his shoulders was covered in tattoos…a twisting network of trees and vines.

The man turned around, and startled when he saw Anne.

"Oh, shit," he said.

Anne was shocked into silence for a moment before she could get a word out.

"Roberto," she said.

"Yeah, hi," Roberto replied. "Sorry, I was…I spilled coffee on my shirt earlier…I didn't think anyone would… lemme just…" He reached over and pulled a plain white cotton t-shirt over his head. A brown stain was spread over the front of it. Anne was tempted to tell him not to put his shirt back on, but then remembered that it was Roberto, and couldn't quite think straight. Her mind raced with a hundred questions. What the hell was he doing here? And when did he start to look like that without a shirt? When did he get those tattoos? Why was he in the bookstore, measuring a wall?

Then it dawned on her.

"You're the architect," Anne finally said.

"Huh?" Roberto asked.

"Cosimo said he had an architect coming to help with the thing. You're the architect he meant."

"Oh. Yeah."

The two looked at one another for a moment. Anne was the first to break the silence.

"How long are you here for?" she asked.

"About two weeks," Roberto replied. Anne watched his eyes flit from her feet to her hips to her hair, before landing on her face again. "It's been a while," he added.

"Yeah," Anne replied. Another silence.

"Let me know if I'm in your way," Roberto said.

"You won't be in my way," Anne replied. "I'm um…I usually do yoga in here in the morning, so I'm…going to do that."

"No problem."

Okay, Anne thought to herself. *Roberto Bonino.*

He was the last man she had ever expected to see in the bookstore again, and she was having trouble orienting herself to the fact of it. It was completely unfair that he was even more good-looking than she remembered. The dark hair and piercing eyes. The crooked nose. The cleft in his chin that he'd always hated. She hadn't seen him since they were teenagers, and now here he was. A man. She glanced up at him again, his (now fully clothed) back to her. Even with a shirt, she could see his muscles working. Damn.

She rolled out her mat as far away from Roberto as possible, and made her way through each pose while she tried not to think about Roberto Bonino and not look at his shoulders while he measured, sketched, and wrote things down.

So of course she thought about him. How could she not? There was so much to think about. They had been best friends for their entire childhoods. She couldn't remember a time before Roberto was in her life. Their families had been friends since before either of them were born. They'd grown up together. Swimming in the creek when they were ten. Mario Kart tournaments when they were thirteen. That time she cried at school in 9th grade because she'd gotten her period and it had stained her pants, and Roberto had frowned with concern and confusion and then offered her a band-aid, which had made her laugh until she wasn't crying anymore. Going to prom in a big group—her and Tyler, Maya and Roberto, Corinne and Devan, Becky and Sean. They'd all gone star-gazing in the park afterward. Anne and Roberto had knocked on their shared bedroom wall to say goodnight to each other, for years and years.

And then there was that awful awful night, when Tom and Gabby got in the car accident, watching Roberto's face crumple, watching his whole body collapse inward. She remembered reaching her hand out to rub his back, and him swatting her hand away.

In the early morning light of the bookstore, Anne shook her head, not wanting to remember that night or anything after it.

But the memories came back anyway. How she'd tried to comfort him, how she'd tried to tell him she was there. How he fell further and further away from her, into some dark place where she couldn't reach him. He had refused to take the hand that she was stretching out to him. He had refused everyone's hands.

He left for Chicago less than a week later, and they

hadn't spoken since. When he moved away, she felt like he took a part of her with him.

Anne had no idea how to feel about any of it. She and Roberto were both twenty-five now, grown-ups and professionals and, she assumed, college graduates. They had always planned on going to college in New York together, and Anne had cried her first week at school, missing him and her mother and the Boninos and Maya and everyone so much it was a physical ache in her stomach.

She tried to concentrate on her breathing as she stretched and moved. Their interaction that morning had been...polite. That was doable. She could be polite to Roberto Bonino for a couple of weeks.

It was only a couple of weeks.

CHAPTER 10

Yoga

ROBERTO

R oberto rubbed the back of his neck and tried to concentrate on taking measurements of this goddamned wall, which he kept needing to re-do because Anne was even more gorgeous than he'd remembered and it was distracting. It was not fair. Those same red curls and those eyes…what was a good word to describe her eyes? Stunning? Shocking? Arresting. She had those arresting green eyes. The same gap between her teeth.

Roberto glanced over her shoulder at where Anne was doing some sort of complicated stretch on her yoga mat. He could see the tiniest amount of cleavage and it was enough to drive him insane. God, her body. He could feel the soft roundness of her hips beneath his hands, could imagine her tilting her head back and sighing as he ran his fingers over her curves…

He shook his head. Hell. *Snap out of it, Bonino,* he thought to himself. *You were kind of an asshole the last time you saw her, and your distant and polite conversation this morning shows that she clearly still thinks you're an asshole, which you actually kind of are, so get your head on straight and do this architect thing and get out of here.*

Besides, Anne had that list. The Plan. She wanted to marry a nice boy and settle down in West Tindale, and that was *not* what he wanted. The thought of staying in this town forever made him feel like his skin was on fire. And he wasn't sure he was a "nice boy." And anyway WHY WAS HE EVEN THINKING ABOUT THIS? He wasn't interested in Anne and she wasn't interested in him. They had a thing when they were kids and now he just thought she was hot and that was it.

At least he thought they had a thing when they were kids. He could be wrong. But no, it was there. They had even held hands that night looking at the stars after prom, even though Maya was his date and Tyler was hers.

Roberto turned back to the wall and his measuring tape. He had not planned on being half-naked during his first meeting with Anne after all these years. But it was seven in the morning. He could barely function enough to get out of bed, but he was trying this thing where he was a responsible adult who did things like get up early and get to work. Cosimo had already gone on a run, showered, and gotten dressed by the time Roberto made it next door to the bookstore. Roberto had stumbled downstairs and promptly spilled more than half of his coffee onto himself. He couldn't bring himself to go all the way backstairs again quite yet.

Roberto glanced over at Anne again. Good god, how was he supposed to concentrate on anything when she was moving like that? He shook his head again and looked down at his notes.

It would be fine. It was only two weeks.

～

ROBERTO REACHED out and moved a curl out of Anne's face. Her lips fell open, and he was hypnotized. Before he could think about it, he was pressing himself against her, the hard planes of his body against the soft curves of hers, his lips pressing insistently against her mouth. He grabbed her waist and lifted her onto the register counter and stepped between her legs, pressing kisses down her neck, along her cleavage, her breath coming in soft moans.

And then they were on the floor, and she was beneath him, her eyes closed, her back arching as he moved inside her. He couldn't believe how good it felt. He couldn't get enough of her.

Music filled the air.

Not sexy, romantic music. Digital, jangling music.

Roberto opened his eyes. He was in his own bed, his alarm a jarring contrast to where his mind had just been.

Dream, Roberto thought. *It was a dream.*

Jesus.

He glanced down and realized his dick was hard in his hand. He laid his head back. He hadn't had a sex dream like that in…well, a while. He reached over to turn his alarm off on his phone. He paused, and then with another glance down at his crotch, pulled up a video to help him finish. Because he was not about to jerk off to the dream he had just had, or to any of its accompanying thoughts or images, as tempting as it was. Because there was nothing between him and Anne anymore, and he was not in her Plan, so it was no use even thinking about it. Fantasizing seemed like a bad idea.

Just gotta take care of this and head downstairs to work.

～

Roberto was feeling vaguely annoyed that apparently he was reverting back to being a teenager just because he was back in the place he'd lived when he was a teenager. He still had the occasional sex dream as an adult, but last night was a lot. After showering, he dragged himself downstairs to where Cosimo was working in the restaurant kitchen. Roberto leaned against the wall as he watched Cosimo chopping vegetables and putting them in plastic bins.

"Hey," Cosimo said.

"Hey," Roberto replied.

"If you're hungry, there's stuff in the kitchen upstairs," Cosimo said.

"Thanks."

"Do you have time to meet with Debbie this morning?" Cosimo asked. "She wants to show you some of our ideas, and do some brainstorming. I think she also had questions for you as the 'Head Architect.'"

"As the Head Architect, that sounds good to me," Roberto replied. "Do you…do you need any help…?"

Cosimo waved him away. "Nah," he said. "You're here to work on the renovation. Besides, I've been doing this on my own for years."

"Right," Roberto said. They were both silent for a moment, and then Roberto left to go next door.

CHAPTER 11

The Rules

ANNE

A nne came downstairs to the bookstore to find her mom and Roberto sitting at a small table, papers scattered over its surface.

"Good morning," Anne said.

"Annie! Come sit with us," Debbie replied.

Anne unlocked the front door and switched the sign to "open," then finally collapsed into a third chair. She'd already done her morning yoga/breakfast/shower routine, and she had only put a little mascara on that morning, as usual. She had been tempted to put a little more effort in, but that would make it seem like she was trying too hard, and she definitely wasn't trying. At all.

"I think we found a name for the café," Debbie said. "Cosimo and I were talking about it yesterday. What do you think of 'Pages and Pasta'?" Anne considered.

"I like it," she said.

"The other idea was 'Spines and Spaghetti.'"

"That…sounds like we put human spines in the food," Anne said. "Like, skeletons."

"Oh, that's a good point," Debbie replied. "And we

won't do that. At least I assume we won't. But anyway, we'll serve more than spaghetti."

Anne laughed and caught Roberto's eye. He met her eyes briefly, and there was a hint of a smile there. They both looked away.

"Pages and Pasta Bookstore and Café," Debbie said, smiling. "Okay! Oh, this will be lovely. Cosimo said something about a blue and gold palette, so you can take that and run with it. I've got to run to the hardware store for a few things, so Annie, while it's slow, you two can get to work." She stood up.

"Wait, us two?" Anne said.

"Yes, you two. You said you'd be willing to help with the new layout and everything. We need your artistic eye for a good floor plan."

Anne frowned. "But I don't know anything about café layouts or floor plans."

"That's why Roberto's going to work with you," Debbie said. "You've both got good eyes, and he's got the structural know-how, and you've got the organization skills —it's a match made in heaven!"

Anne blinked at her mother for a moment, then stole a glance at Roberto. He was diligently sketching something on a piece of paper and ignoring the conversation.

"It doesn't have to be perfect on the first draft," Debbie finally said. "Just sketch out a few ideas together. Make some plans. Brainstorm. We'll all look at it together sometime tonight or tomorrow, whenever you're ready. See you in a few hours!"

"Mom," Anne said. "This isn't what I had in mind when you said you wanted me to help plan things. I thought I'd be picking out paint colors and, I dunno, sketching up new logos."

"You are doing those things. You're also helping

Robbie with the layout. It doesn't make any sense to just pick out paint colors if you also don't know the layout. A space needs flow. Love you!"

And Debbie was out the door.

Anne looked at Roberto, then at the papers spread before them.

"I'll be right back," she said.

When she came back, she held a clean bullet journal in one hand, and a zippered bag full of pens and highlighters in the other. She opened the journal to the first page and wrote "The Rules."

She didn't look up at Roberto as she spoke. "Okay, if we're going to make this work, I think we need some rules."

"Rules? For the café?"

"For us working together," Anne replied. "We haven't spoken in years and when you left, there was…" Anne struggled for a moment to find the right words. "There was a lot of hurt there," she finished. "I don't think either of us is exactly thrilled about this situation, so I think it'd be a good idea to clarify a few things."

"What makes you think I'm not thrilled about this?" Roberto asked.

Anne looked at him. "Are you? Thrilled to be back in West Tindale, after eight years away?"

Roberto looked down and didn't answer. Anne ducked her head over her notebook and took a deep breath.

"Rule one," Anne said as she wrote. "Consult one another before making any decisions regarding the café. Parentheses, purchasing supplies, making plans, advertising, etc., parentheses."

"You don't need to say 'parentheses' out loud," Roberto said.

Anne frowned at him, but there was a hint of a gleam in his eye. "Fine," Anne said, turning back to the journal.

"Rule two," Roberto said. Anne's head snapped up in surprise for a moment, and then poised her pen above the paper, ready to write down what Roberto said.

"We exchange phone numbers but respect one another's space."

Anne wrote it down. "So no calling or texting at ungodly hours, you mean?"

"Yes," Roberto replied.

When she looked back up at him, he was leaning back in his chair, hands behind his head, gazing at her. He stretched, and she caught a glimpse of his stomach, a line of dark hair leading down into his jeans. She quickly turned her focus back down to the journal in front of her.

"Rule three," she said. "Trust in one another's expertise." She wrote it down, then looked up. "That means I won't tell you how to architect, and you won't tell me how to design."

"Fair," Roberto said, smiling. "Anything else, Type A Annie?"

Anne narrowed her eyes at him, then bent over to write in the journal. "Rule four, *Robbie*," she said. "Shirts stay on at all times. Think you can manage that?"

Roberto's smile widened into a grin. "I'll try."

"Okay," Annie said, sitting back. "I guess if we're going to trust one another's expertise, we need to know what that expertise is. I don't know much about architecture. Is your work mostly exterior or interior?"

"Pretty equally both. And your expertise?"

"I'm brilliant at decor and branding and kind of anything visual."

"I think we can make that work. I'll do shapes and you do colors," Roberto said.

"I'm kickass at colors."

"And at organizing," Roberto added, gesturing to the bullet journal.

"And at organizing," Anne repeated, smiling. "Speaking of which…" She opened the bullet journal to a clean page. "I already have some ideas about what we need to keep track of."

CHAPTER 12

Go For a Run

ROBERTO

Roberto sat back and watched as Anne flipped through pages, writing different headings on each one. "Initial ideas." "Possible challenges." "Assignments." "Branding." She bit her lip as she stared into a space and thought for a minute. Watching her mouth, Roberto's mind was suddenly filled with images from his dream last night.

Focus, Bonino. He shifted in his seat. *Think about the work.*

As Anne slowly filled up the pages of the journal with different sections, Roberto glanced down at the papers spread across the table between them. She was definitely more organized than he was, that's for sure. He'd probably drive her insane within a day, if not an hour.

Anne looked over at him. "Okay, tell me what you've got so far."

Roberto looked down, then slowly pushed all of the papers over towards Anne. He had scribbled some measurements into the corner of a page of sketches, made a list of supplies he thought of on an old receipt, and there was the name and phone number of the building code office written on a piece of scrap paper.

Anne raised her eyebrows.

"This is what we've got so far," he said.

Anne looked at the papers and then hung her head in her hands.

"This is like 10th-grade chemistry all over again," she moaned.

"We passed 10th-grade chemistry!"

"Because of *me*," Anne replied.

"I did my part!" Roberto protested. "Besides, I was like fifteen."

Anne looked up at him. "But you're not fifteen now, and this isn't going to work if I have to do all of the heavy lifting."

"Like you could lift anything heavy," Roberto teased. But he was surprised to see Anne just shake her head.

"I'm serious, Roberto," she said. "I'm not going to carry you through this project. You've got to carry your weight. I am not going to let you do that thing where men just expect women to pick up their slack. I refuse to do that."

Roberto blinked in surprise. "Do men do that?"

Anne sighed. "The fact that you even have to ask…"

"I don't know, I'd never heard of it."

"It's definitely a thing." Anne said. "Promise me you'll pull your weight here."

"I promise," Roberto said.

Anne gazed at him for a moment, then rested her elbow on the table and held out her pinky. "Pinky swear?"

Roberto looked at Anne's hand, and then at her face. He rested his elbow on the table across from her. "Pinky swear," he said, and he locked his pinky with hers.

A small electric shiver went through him. Anne's skin

was soft and cool, and he realized with a jolt that it was the first time they'd touched since he'd been back. They hadn't had contact of any kind for eight years, physical contact included. He suddenly felt like there wasn't enough air in the room, and the walls were too close, and his skin wasn't his own. He let go of Anne's hand and stood up quickly.

"Hey, sorry, but I've got to go. What if you brainstormed a bit on your own and we can meet up and clarify some things tomorrow?"

Anne frowned at him, her lips full and soft. The sight of it went right through him, through his chest and down to his groin. *Nope*, he said to himself.

"Sure," she said. "Give me your phone."

Roberto handed it over and Anne entered her phone number. "Text me so I'll have yours," she said, handing the phone back. "If you know what supplies you need for construction stuff, we can add it to my list," she added.

"Got it," Roberto replied. He didn't look back as he walked out the door.

WHEN ROBERTO GOT BACK next door, Cosimo was on his way out.

"Is the restaurant closed?" Roberto asked.

"The restaurant's always closed on Tuesdays. It's our 'day off.'" Cosimo looked at Roberto for a moment. "I'm um…I'm actually going to the cemetery," he said. "I put fresh flowers on mom and dad's grave every week." Cosimo paused. "Wanna come along?"

Roberto could not think of anything he wanted to do less. The thought made him feel like he was being squeezed too tightly on all sides, or like the room wasn't quite big enough. He shook his head. "Nah, go without me."

He felt Cosimo's eyes on him as he looked down at the sidewalk, and finally Cosimo broke the silence. "Okay," he said. "If you go anywhere, lock the door behind you?"

"Yep," Roberto said.

As soon as he was inside, Roberto took the stairs two at a time and headed up to his room. He still felt rattled from his moment of physical contact with Anne. *If that's what touching her PINKY is like, what the hell would more feel like?* he thought to himself. That thought also made him feel claustrophobic. He flopped onto his bed and pulled out his phone, but after a few minutes of scrolling, he couldn't sit still.

He texted Lily.

> ROBERTO: I feel like I'm crawling out of my skin.

He laid back and waited for her to text him back. He stood up and paced. Finally, his phone pinged.

> LILY: Kai says to go for a run.

Roberto grabbed his running shoes as he tapped out his reply.

> ROBERTO: Tell your husband he's a genius.

He ran in the opposite direction from the bookstore. He had gone two blocks before he realized he was running the same route he used to run in high school. His feet had remembered the way without him making a conscious choice about it. West on Grizzly Way, right on First Avenue. Another right at the KOA, then east on Silverview to the school. He used to run it during cross-country in high school—their coach used to give them instructions using the route. He called it "the loop." "Gimme a 10-minute loop!" Or "Bonino, give me two loops!"

He and Tyler and Sean would sometimes run in sync with each other, their footsteps falling into a rhythm. If they were taking it a little slower, sometimes they'd talk about school or girls. He felt his feet hit the pavement today in the same steady beat. He hadn't talked to Tyler or Sean in years. They'd all been pretty good kids…maybe trying a few sips of beer at a party or two, but mostly staying out of trouble. They might still be here in town. Following some plan of their own. Everyone in West Tindale had a plan. It was almost like people followed it without realizing it. Like it got into their blood and made them do things without giving them any say in the matter.

But the thing was that plans didn't mean anything. You could plan everything, do everything right, and it could all fall apart in a matter of seconds. He had planned to work at Jiménez Building Design steadily for years. His parents had planned to live in West Tindale until they retired. And none of it had worked out. So why even bother with the planning part? It was just setting yourself up to be disappointed.

Just keep moving forward. Don't plan. Just keep running.

CHAPTER 13

The Drive

ANNE

Anne rolled over in bed and grabbed her phone. She'd already spent at least twenty minutes remembering every detail of how Roberto had looked without his shirt that first day, and another twenty minutes telling herself to stop thinking about said details. There were things that needed to be done today. Without giving herself time to think about it, she tapped out a quick text to Roberto.

> ANNE: Hey I know this is kind of last minute, but I think it'd be good to go to Silver Falls for supplies today. It's a Friday and Debbie can watch the bookstore. Are you free?

She stared up at the ceiling. After Roberto had disappeared yesterday, she'd completely ignored his "notes" and made her own list of supplies. He could add to it today if he needed to.

Her phone buzzed. Roberto.

> ROBERTO: I'm down. See you in half an
> hour?

Anne reached up and felt her frizzy hair, then replied.

> ANNE: Make it an hour. Meet me in the
> bookstore.

An hour later, Anne grabbed her purse to leave. She refused to think about how much time she had put into her hair and makeup. She also intentionally ignored the fact that she had changed her outfit four different times. Because it really didn't matter if she looked good today or not. It was Roberto, and she'd known him forever, and they hadn't spoken in eight years and they were just running an errand and they weren't even really friends anymore.

Granted, it was an errand with a two-hour commute each way, so it was really an all-day errand, but still. Not enough of a reason to think about how she looked.

When she got downstairs, Roberto was sitting at one of the small tables by the windows. He looked up at her when he heard her walk in. How is it that he could look so good in jeans and a t-shirt? He'd worn jeans and t-shirts plenty of times when they were growing up, but Roberto inhabited his body with an ease and power now, one that had not been there when she'd last seen him.

And geez, those eyes, Anne thought. She mentally shook herself, and walked over to hand Roberto the renovation notebook she'd begun the day before, open to her supplies list.

"I made a list," she said. "If you can think of anything you need to add to it, I left some room."

Roberto frowned and looked over the list. "Doesn't the hardware store in West Tindale have most of this stuff?"

"They have some," Anne said. "But it's more expensive, so I figured if we were going to go down to Silver Falls for some of this other stuff anyway, we might as well get everything there. And honestly, sometimes I just don't have the energy for Hans." Hans owned the hardware store in town, and was notoriously grumpy.

Roberto nodded. "Is he still an asshole?"

"Yep."

Roberto looked down at the notebook again. "Are these…organized by store?"

"Yes?"

"And is each store section organized into sub-sections of similar items?"

"It's more efficient that way."

"And is this…color-coded?" A smile had crept into Roberto's voice.

"Just add what you need to and stop judging me," Anne said.

Between last night and this morning, Anne was remembering how ridiculously disorganized Roberto Bonino was. She hadn't thought about it in years, but it was…bad. Like, "random information scribbled on random pieces of paper" bad. Anne had no idea how he functioned at his actual job. Maybe he had a personal assistant or something. *But,* Anne thought, *he'd better shape up for this project because I am not a personal assistant.* She thought this process might drive her actually crazy. Anne believed thoroughly in organization and planning and color-coding. Roberto apparently believed in just kind of remembering things and jotting other things down now and then. While Roberto scribbled a few things in the journal, Anne pulled out her phone and typed out a quick message to Maya.

> ANNE: If I end up in a padded room somewhere, let the record show that it was probably because of how disorganized Roberto Bonino is.

Maya replied right away.

> MAYA: Did you say Roberto Bonino? The fuck?! Is Roberto back in town?! How do you know this? What the hell?!

In the chaos of the past day or so, Anne realized that she hadn't told Maya anything about Roberto. She typed out another text.

> ANNE: He's the architect Cosimo hired for the renovation. He's here for two weeks. It's weird.

Anne paused, then added:

> ANNE: He got very hot.

Maya's reply was mostly a string of emojis (monkey covering eyes, fire, dancing woman in red dress), and Anne texted that she would share details later. She strolled over to the register where Debbie was sitting, a novel in her hand.

"Heading to Silver Falls today?" Debbie asked.

Anne nodded, opening the cash drawer to grab the bank bag of petty cash and the store credit card.

"Don't spend too much on that," Debbie said.

Anne leaned over and kissed her cheek. "I won't," she replied.

The door to the bookstore opened.

"It's meeeee!" Maya's voice rang out.

Anne looked up and raised her eyebrows at her best friend. But Maya was looking at Roberto, who had just glanced up from the notebook where he was still writing down supplies.

Roberto seemed frozen in place for a moment, then he stood up. "Hey, Maya," he said.

"Hi, Roberto," Maya answered, a friendly smile across her face. "It's been a minute."

"Yeah." Both of them stood there for a moment, and then Maya turned to Anne and Debbie at the register.

"Do you have any more flyers for this month's activities? Ours got lost, so I thought I'd just run across the street and grab another."

"Sure, honey," Debbie said. Anne narrowed her eyes at Maya as she walked towards them. She was 99% sure that Maya's family absolutely did not need another flyer, and that Maya had just made it up as an excuse to come over and see Roberto. The two of them had always had an easy friendship—they'd even gone to senior prom together, as part of their big group of friends. Maya had been hurt by Roberto's leaving, too.

But now, she sauntered casually up to the register and took the flyer from Debbie's hand. As soon as Debbie went back to her book, Maya looked at Anne and mouthed, "Oh my god." Anne glanced over her shoulder at Roberto and then gave the smallest nod.

"Good to see you, Roberto!" Maya said as she walked back towards the door. Roberto lifted a hand in goodbye.

"Text me, Anne," Maya said.

"I will." Anne looked at Roberto. "Ready?" she said.

"Sure."

"I assumed we'd take my car, since you don't have one and Cosimo might need his," Anne said, as they walked toward the back of the store.

"You would be correct," Roberto replied. Anne opened the door of her mother's sedan and started the engine as soon as Roberto had sat in the passenger seat.

The drive was mostly silent for the first twenty minutes. Anne debated about finding a podcast to put on, but they were on the part of the drive where she didn't get good cell phone signal, so it would have to wait anyway. Anne kept thinking of things to say to Roberto and then changing her mind about them. Finally, Roberto cleared his throat.

"So, Cosimo said you got a degree from NYU?"

Anne glanced over at Roberto, then focused her eyes back on the road.

"Humanities," she replied. Another pause. "And you're an architect."

"Yeah," Roberto said. He gripped the lever on the side of his seat and leaned it way back. "I mostly design office buildings."

"Office buildings. Cool. Anything I'd know?" Anne cringed internally. *Anything I'd know.* Like she could name a single office building in the world. The Sears Tower? Did that count? Anne doubted she could name more than five buildings total, and it was almost impossible that one of them would be an office building that Roberto had designed.

"I don't think you'd know any of them," Roberto replied, smiling slightly. "I mostly collaborate with other architects anyway. No one designs office buildings single-handedly."

"Right."

Another awkward pause. Anne searched desperately for another topic of conversation.

"Do you like Chicago?"

"I do. It's got lots of culture. A good nightlife."

"Cool."

"And you still like West Tindale?"

"Yep."

The conversation stalled again. Anne thought back to the days when they were teenagers, when words came easily, and when silence felt comfortable. Now talking felt like pulling teeth and the silence felt like hellfire. Everything Anne could think of to say felt absurd.

She stole another glance at Roberto. He was stretched out on the leaned-back seat, one arm above his head. A small strip of his stomach was visible. Anne turned back to the road. *Concentrate*, she said to herself. *You know how to have a conversation.*

CHAPTER 14

The Car

ROBERTO

"Okay," Anne finally said. "This is ridiculous."

"What is?"

"This," she said. "Maybe we should just start over. Pretend we're strangers."

"We are strangers," Roberto replied.

Roberto thought he saw Anne flinch slightly, which made him feel bad. Finally, she sighed. "I suppose that's true." She paused. "What I'm saying is let's act like this is a first date. But like, in a platonic way. Get to know each other."

"That's the worst part of first dates."

"How many first dates have you been on?" Anne asked, frowning.

"Lots," he said, a little sardonically.

Anne glanced over at Roberto. He met her eyes briefly, then looked away.

"How many second dates?" she asked.

The question caught him by surprise. "Fewer," Roberto replied.

Anne paused before she spoke again, and when she did, Roberto could tell she was doing her best to keep the question as casual as possible.

"Anything serious ever?"

"Once," Roberto replied.

"What happened?"

"She married someone else."

"Oh."

Roberto opened his eyes and moved his seat back so that he was sitting upright. "It's okay, though. It was years after we broke up. She got together with one of my close buddies, and now we're all golden. Lily and I actually work together."

He knew a lot of people didn't really get his and Lily's friendship. In truth, she was the only ex he could imagine being friends with at all. But his and Lily's relationship had fizzled into friendship so gradually that neither of them had even really been broken-hearted about it. Maybe Lily had been—he'd never really asked. But now she was like family. Her and Kai.

"Did you ever…did you ever think about getting married?" Anne asked.

Images swam up in his memory of Anne's father dying, leaving her mother alone. He thought of his own parents, and then of the people he knew in Chicago, wading through divorces and cheating and boredom.

"I hadn't really thought about it," Roberto replied. He was quiet for a moment. "What about you? Did you and Tyler ever get together after high school?"

Anne smiled. "Tyler married Corinne."

"Oh."

Roberto frowned and saw Anne glance over at him. "Did you not know that?" she asked.

"I did not know that," Roberto replied. "Anyone else?"

"Is anyone else married?"

"No, have you dated anyone else."

Anne was quiet for a moment. "I had a boyfriend for a while in New York. Garrett. But we broke up after two years. No hard feelings. I wish him well."

Roberto felt a twinge of something he couldn't quite name. Was it jealousy? Guilt? He felt slightly…left behind. Like he should have at least known that Anne had had a serious boyfriend named Garrett in New York. He wondered what else he didn't know. Maybe a lot of things had changed about Anne and who she was and what she wanted.

Roberto could sense The Plan hanging in the silence between them. College in New York, help run the bookstore, get married and settle down in West Tindale. They had planned to go to college together. But the summer after graduation, he'd withdrawn from NYU and gone to Chicago instead.

He was lost in his own thoughts when Anne spoke again.

"So how did you get into architecture?"

By the time they got to Silver Falls, the air was a little easier between them. Which was good, because it turned out that shopping for supplies was more of an endeavor than they thought it would be. Some items were out of stock, so they had to go to different stores. Some items had to be ordered with a later pickup date, some items couldn't be delivered to West Tindale, some items *could* be delivered to West Tindale but only within a very specific window. And every store was crowded with impatient customers.

Anne's renovation notebook was becoming increasingly

colorful, as she crossed items out, highlighted others, wrote notes on new pages. Roberto had laughed when she pulled her zip-lock pouch of pens and highlighters out of her purse at the counter of the lighting store. She shot him a playful glare and turned her attention back to the notebook.

By 1 p.m., both of them were too hungry to think straight, so they sat in Anne's car and ate burgers while they planned out the rest of their errands. By the time they'd gotten everything done and were ready to head home, it was already 8 p.m.

Anne practically collapsed into the driver's seat. The trunk and the backseat were both so full they could barely see out the rearview mirror.

"Okay," she said. "Let's go." She turned the key.

click

She blinked at the dashboard, then tried turning the key again.

click

"The hell?" she muttered.

click *click* *click*

Nothing.

"We good?" Roberto asked slowly.

"We might not be good," Anne said. She pulled the keys out of the ignition for a moment, then put them back in and tried starting the car again. More clicks, followed by nothing.

"Yeah, that doesn't sound good," Roberto said.

Anne closed her eyes and leaned her head against the steering wheel. "This has been happening for a few months but we just haven't taken it in yet."

"If it's just the battery, a jump should at least get us back to West Tindale."

Anne just nodded.

"I'll see if I can find someone to give us a jump," Roberto said. Without even thinking about it, he started to reach out and rub Anne's back in comfort, but stopped himself. He got out of the car instead.

CHAPTER 15

Silver Falls

ANNE

After failed attempts at a jump start from two different strangers, Anne finally relented and called for a tow truck. There was a repair shop nearby, but at 9:30 at night, no one would be available until the next morning. The tow truck driver gave them a ride to the shop, then helped them both climb down.

"Y'all got someone comin' for ya?" he said.

Anne turned to Roberto. "I didn't even think about that," she said.

"The one time in your life you didn't have a plan," Roberto replied. Anne scowled at him.

The driver pulled a card out of his pocket and handed it over to Anne. "We got vouchers for a discount at a hotel if ya need someplace to shack up for the night," he said. "Good luck, y'all."

Anne watched him drive away, then turned to Roberto, the card still in her hand. They stared at one another in silence for a few moments. Then Anne said, "I'll call Maya," she said.

"If you can't get ahold of her, I'll text Cosimo," Roberto replied.

But there was no answer from either of them. Anne tried Debbie, Devan, the Zhaos, and anyone else she could think of, but every person she called was either unavailable or not answering. Anne sat on the sidewalk and leaned against the building. Roberto looked down at her.

"Let's just get the hotel," he said.

Anne sighed. "I don't know if you noticed that the bookstore isn't exactly flush at the moment, and we just spent thousands of dollars on supplies. I don't want to pay for a hotel, too."

"I'll pay for it," Roberto said. "Besides, we have a discount voucher."

Anne looked at the card in her hand, then sighed again. "Fine," she finally said. "I'll text everyone to let them know we're staying here for the night. Just in case anyone actually looks at their phone and sees any of the dozens of messages we've each sent."

Anne fired off a few texts, then looked back up at Roberto.

"Come on," he said. "The hotel's only a few blocks from here." Roberto held his hand out to help Anne up, and she reached up and took it. Anne almost kept Roberto's hand in hers as they started walking, just out of habit. She pulled her hand away, her skin tingling slightly with the memory of his touch.

Anne told herself that there was a simple explanation for the impulse to hold his hand. Walking side by side with him in the moonlight, Anne was transported back to the dozens (hundreds?) of nights of her youth, walking around West Tindale with Roberto. In summer, they'd all stay out until midnight, sitting on the swings at the park playground and talking. It was usually her and Maya and Devan and Roberto, maybe sometimes a few other friends from school. Maybe they'd see a movie at the one tiny movie theatre in town—the one that only showed one movie at a time, and only on Fridays and Saturdays. Or they'd grab ice cream cones from the Dairy Queen on the corner by the bookstore and just wander.

One night when they were fifteen, it was just Anne and Roberto, wandering through town in the summer night. Anne had seen a shadow pass through the lamplight about a block ahead, and she had instinctively grabbed Roberto's hand, and then just not let it go. And every night for the next two summers, Anne and Roberto held hands as they walked around West Tindale. She never said anything about it, and neither did he, and nothing else happened between them until that night when they were seventeen.

It was colder on this short walk through Silver Falls. The walk was quiet, but when they arrived at the hotel, they found the lobby buzzing with activity. People of all ages were talking in small groups, piles of luggage everywhere.

Roberto leaned over the check in counter. "Hi, we're hoping for a room?" he said. "We've got a discount voucher."

"You guys are in luck!" the hotel employee said, smiling. Her name tag said Rowena. "We just had someone cancel, so you guys can have the very last room in town."

"Oh, we need two rooms," Anne said.

"Good luck," Rowena replied. "Every hotel in town is booked solid. There's a convention downtown and a choir competition *and* a football game. We've been turning people away all night."

Anne frowned. "And you don't know of any other place nearby that has rooms?"

"Folks have had rooms booked from here to Rockbridge for months," Rowena said. "I don't know of any other place that has vacancies."

Anne thought for a moment, then laid her head on the counter and laughed. "I mean, this is straight out of a rom-com. Or a cheesy…Hallmark movie or something. This woman actually said the words 'the last room in town.' I didn't think things like this actually happened." She glanced around. The lobby was full of teenagers laughing and talking loudly, accompanied by a handful of adults who all looked exhausted. In another corner, a group of women in expensive-looking business suits were looking at their phones while they talked in low voices and shot glares at the teenagers. Anne turned to Roberto.

"Wanna try and find another place?" she said. "Or wait for someone back home to come get us?"

Roberto thought for a moment. "I don't know if we'll have any luck finding another room," he replied. "And if we go back to West Tindale now, we'll just have to turn around and come back again almost immediately to come get the car. It makes more sense to just stay here."

She looked at Roberto for a brief moment, then at the floor. "I don't have the energy to try to find someplace different," she finally said. "And I'm exhausted." She turned to Rowena. "How many beds does the room have?"

"Two queens."

Anne looked back at Roberto. "I'm fine with it if you are."

"Works for me," Roberto said.

CHAPTER 16

Bed Preferences
ROBERTO

Roberto followed Anne down the hallway. They didn't have suitcases, and it felt a bit surreal to be following her to a hotel room. He'd accompanied plenty of women to their hotel rooms before, but not Anne. He watched her hips sway as she walked in front of him. She'd piled her hair on the top of her head, and a few strands had come loose at the nape of her neck. Roberto wanted to reach out and brush them away and—

Get it together, Roberto, he thought. *You're not a teenager anymore. You're not in Anne's Plan and you barely became kind of friends again this afternoon so don't go and do something stupid.*

Anne stopped in front of their room and turned to him, leaning her back against the door.

"This one's mine," she said, smiling. "I had a great time tonight. Wanna come in?"

Roberto's brain screeched to a halt. "Huh?" he finally managed.

Anne laughed. "I'm kidding. Relax."

"Oh, right. Ha ha," Roberto said. Anne rolled her eyes

at him, still smiling, then turned and unlocked the door. He followed her into the room, and the door clicked shut behind him. They both stood looking at the beds for a moment. Anne was the first to break the silence.

"It's weird to not have a suitcase," she said.

"Yeah," Roberto replied. He stole a glance at Anne, who was looking thoughtfully around the room. He'd missed her. That's what was really going on. He'd missed Anne Winslow. She turned to him.

"Do you have a bed preference?"

Yours, Roberto's brain said, before he sternly told it to shut up. "I'll take either," he said.

"In that case, I'll take this one!" Anne ran and jumped onto the farther bed, landing on her stomach and bouncing slightly.

Roberto's eyes moved over Anne's wide hips and thighs, the curve of her ass, her strong legs. He could feel himself getting hard, his mind racing through a hundred different scenarios in that bed. "Cool," he finally said. "I'm gonna use the restroom."

He shut the door behind him and glared at himself in the mirror. He turned the sink on and splashed cold water on his face. "Seriously, Bonino," he whispered to himself, "Keep it in your pants. Don't even think about your pants. Think about global warming or something. Keep your head on straight."

He took a few deep breaths. Maybe he'd gotten a little too used to just…getting what he wanted. He didn't really pursue anything with women unless he knew they were already interested in the same thing he was. Which, nowadays, was something casual, sexy, and very very temporary. If there was anything more than that, from either party, he always shut it down before it could get too far.

But this was a little bit more difficult to navigate. Anne had been his best friend for his entire childhood, and then they hadn't spoken in eight years, and now he wanted to do a lot of things to her in that hotel bed, and he knew he really shouldn't do any of them.

Besides, he'd already kissed her once. Even if it was years ago.

Roberto hadn't thought about that night in years. He'd deliberately tried not to. But now with Anne in the other room, her curls in a messy bun, her clothes dipping into the curve of her waist and hugging the swell of her breasts, he felt the same electricity in his bones that he had on that night when they were seventeen.

In the hotel bathroom, Roberto closed his eyes and rested his hands on the counter. He looked down and then looked at his reflection in the mirror. "Cool it, Roberto," he whispered. "You're not seventeen anymore. You've both grown up and you want different things."

He took a deep breath and opened the door.

Anne had gotten up from the bed and was sitting at the small table by the window, bent over the renovation notebook, pens and highlighters already out and lined up. She looked up from her notebook at the sight of Roberto exiting the bathroom.

"Hey," she said.

"Hey, yourself."

"Thanks for paying for the room," Anne said.

"No problem," Roberto replied, flopping onto his bed. Anne was quiet, so Roberto started to pull out his phone, but Anne's voice interrupted his thoughts.

"Did you really not know that Tyler and Corinne got married?"

Roberto looked over at Anne, then shrugged.

"They have a daughter," Anne added. She smiled. "Emily. She's four, and she writes these little poems that she shares at our poetry nights at the bookstore. The last one was about trees."

Roberto smiled. "That's ridiculously adorable," he said.

"It really is," Anne replied. She studied his face briefly. "When we were young…" she started. Roberto felt his heart speed up slightly in the pause, but trained his face to stay neutral. He wasn't sure what she was about to say, but anything about when they were young felt a little fraught.

"You used to want five kids," Anne finally said. "Do you remember that? You had all their names picked out."

Roberto blinked at her. "I…I remember the five kids thing, but I one hundred percent completely forgot that I had their names picked out."

Anne laughed. "I don't remember what they were," she said. "I just remember trying to convince you that five is a lot of kids."

"I definitely agree with you now."

"So you only want one or two now?" Anne said, giving him a teasing smile.

"I'll take one or two, *maybe* three if I like the first ones," Roberto replied.

"A reasonable caveat," Anne laughed.

It was fun to just…banter like this. He'd missed it. He'd missed having it with Anne. But he was also aware of the weight of the subject. You could only joke about marriage and kids for so long before it got serious. And the reality was that there *was* a part of him, deep down, that wanted those things. It scared the shit out of him, and he couldn't figure out how he'd ever be the kind of person who had a wife and kids, but maybe if he found the right person…

someone he could be himself with, who saw all his shit and somehow convinced him that it was worth it, maybe he could someday have the kind of domestic life he had expected for himself when he was younger.

But the chances seemed slim now. He decided to change the subject.

CHAPTER 17

Art and Poetry

ANNE

"How's our list looking?" Roberto asked.

Anne held up the notebook. "Like a mess," she said.

"But like, a functioning mess?"

"That's my whole Tinder bio," Anne joked, setting the notebook back down. "A functioning mess."

Roberto laughed. "I'm pretty sure you're not a mess. You're like, the least 'a mess' person I know."

"Thanks," Anne replied, picking up a highlighter to note something on a notebook page. It had taken a minute, but she liked that she and Roberto had fallen back into the same easy banter they had when they were young. The thought made her smile.

"Are you actually on Tinder?" Roberto asked.

Anne paused. "I have been on Tinder," she said, not looking up.

"And?"

"And what?" Anne replied nonchalantly.

"Any luck?"

Anne looked up at Roberto and paused before answering. "One time, a man in New York called me names that I was not into in his very first message. And on one date I went on, the guy refused to wear a condom, so I left." She watched Roberto blink at her, so she added, "I don't think Tinder is the best place for an introverted feminist."

"Yeah, that's a good point," Roberto said.

"What about you?" Anne asked. "Any luck on Tinder?" Roberto gazed up at the ceiling. He almost seemed to be counting. "Never mind, I don't want to know," she said.

"Yeah, dating apps can be a cesspool and you're not missing out on much."

Anne had a moment of feeling like the least cool kid in school. She had felt the same way a lot when she'd first moved to New York. It wasn't necessarily that she wanted to have success on dating apps, but maybe she wanted to be the kind of person who could. Or the kind of person who had. But she wasn't. It made her feel deeply uncool. She had felt the same way at NYU, like she was just a green, provincial homebody from a tiny Montana town. Anne didn't know what Roberto's life was like in Chicago, but she had the feeling it was not as…quiet. As her life had been. As her life was. It was like he'd outgrown her.

"Dating apps can't be a complete cesspool or no one would use them," Anne said. "Maya uses them all the time and she's not a cesspool kind of human."

"Oh, but I am," Roberto replied, smiling.

Anne wasn't sure what to reply. The Roberto she used to know was not a "cesspool kind of human," but that was years ago. She wasn't sure what kind of human he was now.

"So," Roberto said, flopping onto the bed.

"So," Anne replied. She looked up at him. He was scrolling through his phone. The sight was so deeply familiar, it seemed strange that she hadn't seen him do it for almost a decade. Between the last time she watched him scroll through his phone and now, there had been generations of phones. It suddenly seemed ridiculous that they hadn't seen each other the whole time. "So here's a question," she said.

"Shoot," Roberto replied, not looking up from his phone.

Anne was still debating about asking, but the question came out before she could second guess herself. "Why haven't you been back home in all these years?"

Roberto shrugged. "Didn't have a reason to come back."

Anne felt her throat tighten in spite of herself. *Not Cosimo? Not Debbie? Not me?* she wanted to ask. But she swallowed those thoughts down.

"And why Chicago?"

Roberto shrugged again. "Got accepted to a school there."

You also got accepted to NYU, Anne thought, but she didn't say anything. She sat cross-legged on her bed. "I've always wanted to go to Chicago," she said. "So many famous authors lived there. And there are so many art museums. Have you been to any of the art museums since you moved to Chicago?"

Roberto looked up and put down his phone. "Oh my god, Annie, you would love Chicago."

"Yeah?" Anne smiled. Her heart leaped a little at her nickname on Roberto's lips. It was like a light being turned on, one that had been off for years.

"The Art Institute of Chicago is insane." Roberto sat up. "I can't believe it took me so long to go there. You're going to hate me for this—I didn't go until like, last year. I spent hours there the first time I went. Their impressionism wing is just huge. They've got all these Monets and Van Goghs, and that one Moulin Rouge painting by that guy whose name I can never remember."

"Toulouse-Lautrec?"

"That's the one. And I stood in front of the Sunday in the Park Seurat painting for like an hour."

"Did you ever have a Ferris Bueller's Day Off Day?" When they were teenagers, they had made a plan of one day going to Chicago and spending the day doing all the things from the movie. Rent a convertible and joy-ride, visit the Sears tower, have lunch at a very fancy restaurant, watch a baseball game at Wrigley Field, visit the Art Institute of Chicago, watch (or join) a parade.

Roberto looked at her. "Damn," he said. "I had completely forgotten about that."

"How could you forget about that?! It's all you talked about junior year of high school!"

"I dunno, I was just…focused on other things."

"Right," Anne said, looking down.

"But there's so much good art all over Chicago," Roberto said. He told her about the other works he had seen, his eyes lighting up when he talked about a sculpture garden he had visited. Anne felt a fire kindling in her chest, watching him. Half of her wanted to push the heat of it down, and the other half of her liked the warmth.

CHAPTER 18

Poetry and Art

ROBERTO

Most of the time when Roberto talked about art, he could see people's eyes glaze over a little bit. Every now and then, he'd talk shop with another architect who was into it, but Roberto generally kept his artsy talk to himself.

There was also probably some part of him that could still hear the echoes of growing up in West Tindale, being in middle school and having other kids accuse him of being gay because he liked pottery class. But he couldn't help that he liked pottery class. And it's not that being gay would have been a problem, but middle school is rough for everyone and he didn't want to be teased for anything, let alone something that was untrue.

Anne shifted on the other bed, stretching her legs out. "So what made you choose architecture?" she said.

Roberto thought for a moment. "This is going to sound disgustingly artsy, but I like the way that shapes can tell a story. The way the weight and texture of a three-dimensional object can make you feel things. Architecture is shapes and weights and angles that you can step inside of.

If you have to have four walls and a roof, I like when they make you feel something."

Anne smiled. "I like that," she said.

"What about you?" Roberto said. "Why did you choose Humanities?"

"Because I couldn't choose between art and music and poetry and philosophy and history."

"That sounds like you," Roberto said, smiling. "Did getting the degree narrow it down at all?"

"Not at all. And living in New York, being surrounded by all of it, didn't help."

"Did you like New York?"

Anne laid back and looked at the ceiling. "There were things I loved about New York," she said. "I loved that it felt like the center of the universe. I loved that at any given moment, I was only a few blocks away from a poetry reading or a play or an art museum. I met so many interesting people and saw so many interesting things. It was like…it was like suddenly stepping into the middle of, this is going to sound weird, but it was like living inside the electricity of a brain. Like being in the command center of the whole world. West Tindale is more like a steadily beating heart. I'd spent my whole life in the heart of the world. So being in the brain instead was exciting. It made me feel like I was electric, too."

Roberto was seized with a sudden urge to lean forward and pull Anne into his arms. He laid back instead. "That sounds amazing."

"It was. But after a few years, it got tiring. There are some people who move to New York and feel immediately at home, like their bodies just lock into the rhythm of the city. But I can only do it for so long before I start to feel out of sync."

"Got West Tindale in your blood?" Roberto teased.

"I can't help it," Anne said. Her voice was tinged with a small ache, and Roberto immediately felt guilty.

"I don't think that's a bad thing," he added.

Anne had always spoken in poetry, for as long as he'd known her. But there was a clarity to her words now that he hadn't recognized before. Roberto wasn't sure if it was new—if it was something that she had developed in the years they'd been apart, or if it had always been there, and he just hadn't seen it. He couldn't think of a way to ask her. So he searched for another question instead.

"Do you ever think about going back to New York? Just to visit?"

"All the time," she said. "I think I'd love to visit a big city for a few days out of every year. Or maybe longer, I don't know. I've gone back to New York just about every year since leaving, but I'd love to include other cities. Paris, Rome, Vienna." She smiled.

God, he'd missed that smile. There was something luminous about it. When Anne smiled, there was a gentle sort of glow around her. Watching her now, he had the vague sensation of melting, which was probably bad news.

"You've talked about going to Paris since you found out it exists," Roberto said. "I can't believe you haven't gone yet."

Anne looked at him for a moment. "Yes, well, trips to Paris aren't exactly cheap. And the bookstore doesn't pay me nearly enough to make European getaways a regular part of my life."

Roberto had a slight sinking feeling. He wasn't a millionaire, but his salary at the architecture firm probably was enough for a European getaway. He hadn't thought about how different his life was now.

"Sorry," he said. "That was rude."

Anne shrugged. "It's fine. I knew when I got my degree

that it wouldn't pay the bills. Scholarships and grants made it possible for me to go to school, and I got the degree because I care about the arts and wanted to give myself a few years to just…be surrounded by them. In a way that I'm not in West Tindale. I love West Tindale with my whole heart, but it's not exactly cultured."

"That's true," Roberto said.

"My time in New York was a sort of gift to myself. Something I could do just for me, before I settle down."

Roberto looked at Anne for a moment. "This is a pretty personal question," he said, "so don't feel like you have to answer. But…do you really want to settle down in West Tindale? Or are you just doing it because you feel like you have to?"

Anne was quiet while she thought about it. "I really do want to settle down in West Tindale. It's part of The Plan. But it's also where my family is, and was. And I really do love it there. I love the park, and I love the bookstore. And the bookstore is a part of my family's story, and I want to add my own chapter to it."

Roberto nodded.

"Plus, I can do artistic things wherever I am," Anne added.

"That's probably why Debbie and Cosimo threw us both together on this," he finally said.

"Probably."

CHAPTER 19

Ghost Hunters

ANNE

"Hey," Anne said. "Have you figured out if we can knock that wall down between the bookstore and the restaurant?" she asked.

"Logistically, it should be easy. We've just got to wait for permits. But there doesn't seem to be any electrical or plumbing in that wall, so we're good to knock it down."

"And it's…structurally sound? Like the ceiling won't collapse or anything?"

Roberto shrugged slightly. "I hope not," he said.

Anne raised her eyebrows at him. "I feel like we should maybe know for sure if the ceiling will collapse or not before we take a sledge hammer to a wall."

"The ceiling will not collapse." There was a glimmer in Roberto's eye.

"Are you making fun of me?"

"No," Roberto said, smiling.

"It is perfectly reasonable to want to know if the ceiling will collapse before knocking down a wall!"

"I never said it wasn't!"

Anne was tempted to throw a pillow at him, but it felt

juvenile, so instead she sat up and swung her legs over the side of the bed so that she was facing him.

"Okay, well, I made a to-do list for when we get back," she said. "And even though we haven't finalized the ground plan yet, I'm 98 percent sure that whatever we do will involve taking down at least part of that wall. So here's what I'm thinking." She stood up and sat next to Roberto on his bed, bringing her notebook with her.

"After the fucking car gets fixed and we get back into town, we unload supplies to the backroom of the bookstore. We'll have to clear the table and chairs and a few other things from that room, but I think it will work as a 'war room' while we renovate. What?" Anne realized that Roberto was looking at her.

"I just don't think I've ever heard you say 'fucking' before."

"I've said 'fucking' before."

"I haven't heard it."

They looked at each other for a moment, before Anne turned back to the notebook. "Well, I say 'fucking' now," Anne finally said. "If you check on the permits for knocking down that wall, then we can finalize the ground plan, and make more detailed to-do lists from there."

"Ever Efficient Anne," Roberto said. "What if we come up with a ground plan now?"

"Right now?"

Roberto shrugged. "What else are we going to do tonight?"

Anne's head was suddenly filled of plenty of other things they could do in that hotel room tonight, but she shoved those thoughts away.

"Okay," she said. She stood and grabbed the hotel stationary and sat at the table. Roberto came and joined her.

"We can make a plan as if we're knocking down that wall, and have a backup plan just in case it turns out that we can't."

"Look at you, Roberto Bonino," Anne smiled. "Making plans."

"Shut up."

～

IT WAS ALMOST midnight when they finished sketching, brainstorming, and writing out their ideas. By the time they both sat back from the table, they had a solid plan, and a few backup ideas.

Roberto ran his hands through his hair. "I fucking hope we can knock down that wall. This will be pointless otherwise."

"Hey, since when do you say 'fucking'?" Anne laughed.

"Oh, I've said 'fucking' for a long time, babe."

Anne felt butterflies at the use of the word "babe," which she promptly told to stop fluttering.

"Fair," she said. She glanced at the time on her phone. "Should we...go to bed?"

Roberto shrugged. "Honestly, I'm not tired." Roberto glanced around the room. "Wanna watch TV or something?"

"Sure," Anne said.

She glanced over at the rest of the room. The TV was pointed towards her bed at such an angle that it would be pretty impossible for Roberto to see unless he was on her bed.

Anne stood up and approached the TV. "Does this thing...adjust?" She asked. Roberto stood and joined her as she reached behind the TV. It wouldn't budge. Anne glanced between the TV and her bed.

"You are invited to sit on my bed for viewing reasons," she said, not looking at him as she walked towards the bed.

"Thank you," Roberto said, a smile in his voice.

Anne climbed onto the bed and fluffed the pillows behind her back. Roberto watched her for a moment, then grabbed a few pillows from his bed and climbed in beside her. There was some adjusting of legs, some shifting of shoulders. Both of them were careful not to touch, not to cross over the imaginary line into one another's territory. It took a few moments for both of them to get settled. When they finally were, Anne looked up in frustration.

"Dammit. Remote," Anne said. She pointed towards the TV, where the remote was sitting.

"Language, Annabelle!" Roberto said, smiling.

Anne looked at him, then let out a surprised laugh. "Oh my god," she said. "No one has called me Annabelle in years."

Roberto stood up and grabbed the remote, then handed it over. "Pick something good."

Anne flipped through channels for a moment. "Ghost Hunters! I fucking love Ghost Hunters! How do you feel about Ghost Hunters?" she turned to Roberto.

Roberto smiled. "I fucking love Ghost Hunters," he replied.

Two and a half episodes later, the boundaries between their separate sides of the bed had relaxed slightly. They still weren't touching, but Anne had slid down onto the pillows, so that she was lying on her side, her legs curled and her knees almost brushing against Roberto's legs. He had slid down slightly too, so that he was more laying on his back than sitting up, his hands behind his head, his ankles crossed.

"Did it ever occur to anyone that it might be the radio playing stuff in that tunnel?" Roberto said. They'd both been commentating, although some of it had been Roberto teasing Anne about jumping when something surprising happened. ("How do you still scare so easily!?")

"I was about to say the same thing! It's below a damn radio station!"

"A '*fucking*' radio station," Roberto said.

"A fucking radio station," Anne repeated. They watched in silence for a few more moments. Then a screech came from the tunnel on screen and Anne jumped again, this time letting out a small yelp.

"Seriously, Annabelle!" Roberto laughed.

"I can't help it!" Anne said. "It's a reasonable survival tactic!"

"What the hell are you talking about?"

"Humans are *supposed* to be startled by danger! If we were cavemen, I'd survive so much longer than you. I'd noticed the danger and jump and then run away like a reasonable human being," Anne said.

"I'd survive by brute strength," Roberto replied.

Anne looked over at him, and he grinned and flexed his biceps. She rolled her eyes, even though the rest of her body was having a different reaction. "Okay, but you wouldn't need brute strength if you were aware of the danger around you and could just avoid it," she said.

"Yeah, but I wouldn't need to avoid the danger if I could just fucking destroy it. I could just tear that saber-toothed tiger limb from limb," Roberto said.

"You could not do that."

"Oh, I could. Feel this." Roberto flexed again and Anne laughed.

"That's the most juvenile attempt at showing off that I have ever witnessed."

"Ouch, Annabelle."

Anne grinned. Her phone chimed on the nightstand next to Roberto. "Wanna hand me my phone?" she said.

"No, I don't think I will," Roberto said, scooting further down so he was lying flat on the bed. "My pride is too deeply wounded."

Anne rolled her eyes. "Fine," she said, and leaned over to pick up her phone.

When it was in her hand, she went to return to her side of the bed, but she turned her head slightly and realized just how close she was to Roberto. She froze, her face hovering inches from his. They looked at each other.

"Hi," Roberto said quietly.

"Hi," Anne replied.

I could so easily just close the distance between us and kiss him right now, Anne thought. Or rather, her brain said something like "want kiss move close kiss please do sexy hot" because she wasn't quite able to form a coherent sentence.

Anne wasn't sure how long she stayed frozen in place like that, but finally Roberto broke the silence. "Phone?" he asked.

"Huh?" Anne replied. Her brain was still not quite functioning.

"Who texted you?"

"Oh. Right." Anne grabbed her phone and retreated to the safety of her side of the bed, reading the message on the screen.

"Maya says we're on our own." Anne said. "Considering the fact that it's two in the morning, I don't blame her." She looked over at the television screen, where the credits for the episode were rolling. She turned to Roberto. "Should we go to sleep?"

"Sure," Roberto said, lifting himself up and standing to stretch. He grabbed the remote and turned the TV off. "See you in the morning, I guess?"

"Yes. And also right now. Don't forget rule four," Anne added.

"Rule four?"

"Shirts stay on at all times."

Roberto grinned. "If you insist."

Anne's stomach flipped and she settled down into the blankets. "Okay, so uh…good night?"

"Good night."

CHAPTER 20

Back in West Tindale
ROBERTO

Roberto and Anne took turns using the cheap plastic toothbrushes and tiny tube of toothpaste in the bathroom. Neither of them had pajamas, so afterward, Roberto simply climbed into his bed and turned his back to Anne. Normally, he'd pull off his jeans and shirt, but Anne had reminded them of the rule about keeping clothing on.

What had come over him in that moment when Anne was hovering above him? He'd wanted so desperately to kiss her. He'd wanted to tangle his hands into her hair and pull her towards him and—

He cut himself off. Hadn't he already given himself a stern talking-to earlier in the night? He closed his eyes, then pulled out his phone and opened the notes app, making sure the light was dim enough to not disturb Anne in the other bed. He began typing.

REASONS YOU SHOULD NOT KISS ANNE
WINSLOW
1. YOU ARE GOING BACK TO CHICAGO IN LIKE
A WEEK AND A HALF.
2. YOU HAVEN'T SPOKEN IN EIGHT YEARS.
3. YOU'RE NOT SURE IF YOU EVER WANT TO
GET MARRIED, AND SHE DOES WANT TO GET
MARRIED.
4. YOU DO NOT WANT TO LIVE IN WEST
TINDALE, AND SHE DOES.
5. YOU BARELY BECAME FRIENDS AGAIN,
MAYBE, SO DON'T FUCK IT UP.

Roberto closed his eyes again. Maybe he was over-thinking this. The list he had just made should be labeled "Reasons You Should Not Date Anne Winslow." He could kiss a girl without dating her. Hell, it's what he usually did. And maybe Anne would be fine with just making out. A one-time thing. Maybe even more than making out? To just…get it out of their systems. A hookup to let off some steam and then he could go back to Chicago and she could find a nice boy to marry and stay in West Tindale with and that would be that.

But it probably wouldn't just be a hookup, a voice inside him whispered. He thought back again to that night in his basement, and the cemetery afterward, then tightened his jaw and willed himself to go to sleep.

The car turned out to be an easy fix, and they were on the road by 1 p.m. the next day, though both Roberto and Anne looked a little worse for wear. They'd slept in their clothes and Anne's makeup was slightly smudged, a sight that felt intimate to Roberto in a way he couldn't help but like a little bit. Anne was immediately back in Planning Mode.

"When we get back, let's unload into the war room and then go our separate ways for the day. Will you call to find out about knocking down the wall? I'll talk to Mom and Cosimo about when the best time to demo would be."

Roberto smiled. "Look at you with the jargon. 'Demo.'"

"I've watched enough home renovation shows to know the jargon," Anne replied.

~

A FEW DAYS LATER, Roberto strolled over to the bookstore just as Anne was about to lock up. She smiled at him and opened the door.

"Hey," she said.

Roberto held up a sledgehammer. "Wanna do some demo?" he asked.

Anne's eyes widened. "Did you get the permits?"

Roberto nodded and grinned.

"And Mom and Cosimo can still run the bookstore and restaurant with the wall gone?"

Roberto nodded again.

"Lemme change my clothes!" Anne said, then turned around.

Roberto stepped inside and walked towards the wall separating the bookstore from the restaurant. The small hole Debbie had made earlier was still there. He pushed furniture out of the way and began covering everything with plastic sheets. The way Anne had greeted him made him feel like they really were friends again. After bonding over Ghost Hunters in the hotel, they'd worked easily together over the past few days. Things were maybe not the way they had been when they were younger, but it was enough. Even if he wasn't quite sure where to step, he felt like the ground was solid beneath him.

Anne came bounding down the steps, wearing jeans and an old t-shirt. She was in the process of sweeping her hair into a messy bun on the top of her head. Roberto fought a smile as she approached. Maybe the ground wasn't quite solid beneath him, but the tilt sure was fun.

"Do we have eye protection or anything?" she asked.

Roberto picked up a bag and reached into it, then handed Anne some clear plastic goggles, a face mask, and some heavy-duty gloves. She put them on without hesitation and reached for the sledgehammer.

"Are you sure you don't want me to do it all?" he teased, putting on his own gloves and goggles.

Anne glared at him.

"I have always wanted to sledgehammer a wall and you will not deprive me of this experience," she replied.

Roberto put on his face mask, then stepped back and gestured towards the wall.

Anne held the sledgehammer aloft, the looked at Roberto.

"Are we *sure* this won't cause the entire building to collapse?" she asked.

"Ninety-nine-point nine percent sure."

"That point one percent, though…"

"Come on, Annabelle."

Anne lowered the sledgehammer and frowned. "Wait, where are Cosimo and Mom anyway? Shouldn't they be a part of this?"

"Technically, they already are, since they started the process with a hammer way before you and I got involved. Your mom said she was getting coffee with a friend and Cosimo said he had a date, so it's just us."

"A date?!"

"Swing the hammer, Annie!"

Anne lifted the sledgehammer and with a guttural cry, swung it hard into the wall.

The drywall cracked with a loud clattering sound, and chunks of the wall fell to the ground, hitting the plastic.

Anne stared at the spot for a moment and then let out a surprised laugh. She looked up at Roberto, her eyes wide, a slow grin spreading across her face. Roberto smiled back and grabbed the other sledgehammer.

"Take turns," he said. "One swing each. Ready?"

Anne crouched slightly and raised the sledgehammer again. "Ready," she replied.

CHAPTER 21

An Erotic Sledgehammer Experience

ANNE

Anne watched as Roberto swung the sledgehammer into the wall. Another cascade of dust and drywall clattered onto the plastic laid over the floor. *There are those damn fucking muscles again*, she thought, looking at him. Anne hadn't spent much of her life going for muscular guys. If she had to define a type for herself, it was definitely more of the "skinny guys who wore flannels and carried around moleskin notebooks" type. But she couldn't deny that Roberto was pleasant as hell to look at. And he did have so many of the features she'd always found attractive. That strong jawline, the good hair, the gorgeous eyes. She even liked his crooked nose. He used to tell people that he broke it in a fight as a kid, but Anne knew it had just always been that way. And he was artistic in his own way. The way he talked about architecture was almost as hot as his shoulders were. He—

"Your turn," Roberto said. Anne's thoughts were interrupted. She looked at the wall and swung hard.

It was ridiculously satisfying.

She watched Roberto swing, then she lifted the sledgehammer and swung again. Adrenaline coursed through her with every movement. The hole in the wall grew bigger and bigger. They fell into a rhythm, switching positions when they needed to. They knocked out drywall and wood panels, leaving the studs in place, revealing more of the restaurant on the other side.

Within minutes, Anne was sweating, strands of hair sticking to her neck, drywall dust settling on her arms. On her next swing, she let out a guttural yell.

"Hyyuuugh!"

Roberto paused and looked at her, then let out his own yell as he swung. "Hyyuuugh!"

It was like some animalistic thing had taken over Anne's body. She swung harder, whole chunks of the wall coming down as she yelled. With every swing, her yells became louder, Roberto joining in on his swings, the two of them creating a new rhythm, one of cries and shattering drywall.

"Hyyuuugh!" *Clatter!*

"Hyyuuugh!" *Clatter!*

"Hyyuuugh!" *Clatter!*

The wall was nearly gone. Anne took one last enormous swing, letting out the loudest cry yet. "RRRAAAAU-UUUGGHHH!" A final cascade of drywall and wood crumbled down. She dropped the sledgehammer and whipped off her face mask and goggles. She stood panting, then looked over at Roberto.

He had taken his goggles and face mask off, too, and he was standing and looking at Anne, breathing heavily, his chest rising and falling. Sweat dripped down the sides of his face. He was covered with white powdery dust from the drywall, and his arms were flexed and glistening as he held the sledgehammer.

Something crackled in the air between them. Anne

wasn't sure how long they stood there like that, breathing hard, looking at each other. Finally, Roberto dropped his sledgehammer and took off his gloves. He ran a hand through his hair, and watching him made Anne's entire body buzz with electricity.

"Are you good?" he said.

Anne was still catching her breath. She looked at Roberto. "Yeah."

Another pause. Roberto seemed to be debating something in his head. He looked at the ground, then looked back up at Anne, his blue eyes sending sparks through her.

Anne looked at him. "Yeah," she finally said again.

"Good," Roberto replied. He took off his gloves and walked through the newly opened hole in the wall to Bonino's Family Restaurant, not looking behind him, and disappeared around a corner.

Anne stood for a few moments, looking at the hole in the wall, at the place where Roberto had disappeared. She felt disoriented, like she'd been walking up a set of stairs and missed a step. It was taking her a moment to find her balance again. She pulled off her gloves and dropped them on the ground, onto the crumbled drywall around her feet. She was still slightly out of breath.

She thought back to the way she'd yelled when wrecking the wall, and felt slightly exposed. It felt a little like what Maya called "a vulnerability hangover"…that slightly embarrassed feeling you get sometimes after telling someone something private about yourself. There was an uncertainty, but also a lovely sense of intimacy.

But the idea of intimacy with Roberto didn't quite feel embarrassing. It felt…exciting. Like a private gift. Like something she used to have before, and something she wanted to keep having. Her mind flooded with the image of him standing opposite her, swinging the sledgehammer, his determined face, his grin as he'd watched her. It sent thrills through her.

Oh. *Oh.*

Shit.

Anne turned and headed back upstairs. She grabbed her phone and typed out a quick S.O.S. to Maya.

> ANNE: Just had a slightly erotic sledgehammer experience knocking a wall down. I might have a thing for Roberto Bonino...?

She put her phone down and grabbed a towel, then turned on the shower so that she could stand under the water and think about her recent revelation. By the time Anne had gotten out of the shower, she had fourteen texts and two missed calls from Maya.

> MAYA: YOU HAVE ALWAYS HAD A THING FOR ROBERTO BONINO.

> MAYA: "Slightly Erotic Sledgehammer Experience"?????

> MAYA: What wall?

> MAYA: Of course you have a thing for Roberto Bonino. You have since middle school. And have you seeeeeen grown up Roberto Bonino?

> MAYA: I need to know more about this Slightly Erotic Sledgehammer Experience.

> MAYA: Anne.

** MISSED CALL: MAYA CLARK **

MAYA: Anne, you cannot text me about a Slightly Erotic Sledgehammer Experience and then NOT REPLY TO MY TEXTS.

MAYA: I need to know how the Sledgehammer Experience was Slightly Erotic because I don't know what the fuck you mean.

MAYA: Like, I trust you, I BELIEVE that the experience was erotic, I just don't know what you mean.

MAYA: Did you knock over a wall with a sledgehammer? Or did Roberto knock over the wall with a sledgehammer? Was he shirtless? Were you naked?

MISSED CALL: MAYA CLARK

MAYA: What the hell Anne

MAYA: I have been wanting to talk to you about how hot Roberto Bonino is for days and you are ruining my life by not answering my calls or my texts

MAYA: RUINING.

MAYA: MY.

MAYA: LIFE.

MAYA: If you don't reply to my texts/calls within half an hour I am sending Roberto Bonino a picture of my tits

Anne laughed, then called Maya. Maya didn't even say hello, she just yelled.

"Aaaauuuuggggghhhh!"

"I'm sorry, I was in the shower!" Anne replied.

"Okay, first explain what the fuck you mean by a 'Slightly Erotic Sledgehammer Experience.'"

"I mean that it was like…deeply cathartic. But also, we were both sweating and—"

"Pause. What the fuck were you sledgehammer-ing?"

"The wall between the restaurant and the bookstore," Anne said.

"Okay, continue. You were sweating…"

"We were both sweating and swinging these sledge-hammers and sort of yelling? Like…crying out?"

"This just sounds like demolition."

Anne sighed. "Maybe you had to have been there."

"If I had been there, I don't think it would have been erotic."

"That's true," Anne laughed.

"So?" Maya said. "You have a thing for Roberto Bonino? Are you finally admitting it? Do you want to ride him until he can't walk and have a bunch of his babies and live happily ever after?"

Anne thought for a moment. "Here's what I know," she finally said. "He's objectively one of the most attractive people I have ever met in real life."

"Correct."

"Like, I'd have to be either a total lesbian or completely asexual to not be attracted to Roberto Bonino."

"Also correct. What about the rest of it?"

"Yes, I probably do want to ride him until he can't walk."

"And have a bunch of his babies and live happily ever after?"

Anne didn't answer right away.

"Anne?"

"I don't think Roberto Bonino fits into The Plan."

"Fuck The Plan!"

"I can't fuck The Plan, Maya. I don't *want* to fuck The Plan."

"No, you just want to fuck Roberto Bonino."

"Probably."

Maya sighed. "Okay, well, can The Plan include just having super hot sex with Roberto Bonino and then he can go back to Chicago and you never see him again?"

"That doesn't sound like the best idea…"

"Come ON, Annie. He is a Scorpio sun and a Taurus moon. That's like…sex god status. Like, mind-bending, dimension-hopping sex. I'm talking—"

"I get it," Anne laughed.

"Plus, we've all been waiting for you two to make it since we were all like, thirteen years old. It's very unsatis-fying to the rest of us."

Anne had a brief flash of memory from that night in the cemetery.

"Yeah," Anne replied. "I know. I'll think about it. For your sake," she joked.

"Good," Maya replied.

CHAPTER 22

The Shower and Getting Drunk

ROBERTO

After leaving Anne downstairs with the wreckage of the wall, Roberto took the stairs two at a time, tore off his clothes, and stepped into the shower. If he didn't do something about his thoughts immediately, he was pretty sure he was going to explode. Just the sight of Anne standing there, looking at him with fire in her eyes, her hair damp on her forehead…it was sending his mind (and his groin) into chaos. For god's sake, it wasn't even that sexual of a situation. All she was doing was standing there, fully clothed and covered with drywall dust. But something about her full lips and heaving chest and intense eyes had made him hard enough to pound nails.

Roberto closed his eyes and let the hot water of the shower pour over him, down his neck and over his chest. Back in the hotel bathroom in Silver Falls, he'd told himself that it would be a bad idea to jerk off to thoughts of Anne. But he was losing his mind, and it seemed necessary right at that moment to do something about it.

After a few minutes, he leaned forward against the shower wall and gripped his cock in one hand, pumping it slowly once. He thought of the way Anne had sounded, swinging the sledgehammer into the wall, her wild cries. There had been something so vulnerable about it. It made him feel like he was watching something deep and honest. His mind created a different picture of her crying out, this time in his bed, her hair clinging in damp strands to the sides of her face, her eyes closed.

He ran his thumb over the head of his cock. It had been wet before he'd even gotten into the shower. He imagined Anne's body over him, straddling him, her head thrown back as she rode him hard.

It's not like he had *real* feelings for Anne. She was just…stupidly attractive. He told himself that all of this was just sexual tension. Just something he had to work out of his system real quick. He imagined moving his hands over her tits, down her sides. He could almost feel his fingers sinking into her full hips as he pictured her moving against him.

The thought made his cock twitch in his hand, and he stroked himself faster. God, he wanted to make her come. It's not just that he wanted to come. He wanted to make Anne come, to make her feel as good as she made him feel. He thrust into his hand as he imagined lifting his hips to push himself deeper into Anne, imagined the sounds she would make. Something wild and vulnerable, like the way she'd cried out while they knocked the wall down together. If he had her in his bed, if she was there, riding him hard, he would reach up with one thumb and draw tiny circles on her clit while she got what she needed from his cock.

Roberto moaned through gritted teeth as he moved his hand up and down his dick under the hot water of the shower. He imagined Anne raking her nails down his chest as she sped up, getting closer. He could picture her biting her lip, squeezing her eyes shut, then gasping as they came together. The thought of her crying out his name as she climaxed was enough to send him over the edge.

Roberto let out a guttural groan as he came hard, the results of his lust in streaks against the shower wall. It took him a few minutes to catch his breath. He leaned his head back and let the water cascade over him.

"Fuck," he whispered. He looked down, then reached for the soap.

THE NEXT MORNING, Roberto went down to the kitchen where Cosimo was working and leaned over the counter. "Hey," he said.

"Hey," Cosimo replied.

Roberto had that old claustrophobic feeling again, the one that made him feel anxious and jumpy. If he was in Chicago, he'd go to a club or start swiping through Tinder to distract himself, but neither of those things were available to him at the moment. There were no clubs, and probably no one in West Tindale he could connect with on Tinder. Besides, he could vaguely hear Lily's voice in the back of his head, telling him that being in West Tindale was supposed to be like rehab, an isolated place to get his shit together.

But the truth was that he was *tired* of rehab. Sometimes a guy needed a break. Roberto looked at his brother and then spoke. "Hey, is there any place in town to get drinks?" he asked.

Cosimo blinked. "There's the bar across the street."

"Wanna go tonight?"

"Uh…sure?" He frowned. "Have we ever gotten drinks together?"

"I don't think so. I don't think sneaking a couple of beers when we were teenagers counts."

"I'm down."

"9 pm? After you close up?"

"Yeah."

Roberto spent the rest of the day on his laptop upstairs, finalizing architecture plans and not thinking about Anne Winslow.

Later that night, roughly two hours after they'd gotten to the bar, Roberto was truly and actually shit-faced. He couldn't quite remember how many drinks he'd had. He had stopped counting after six. Maybe they made them stronger than he remembered in West Tindale. Then again, he'd never gotten drunk in West Tindale. His tongue felt a little bit too big for his mouth, and he was vaguely aware that he was slurring slightly. But at the moment, he was concentrating on keeping the bar in front of him from tilting. He knew he needed it to stop tilting before he could stand up properly.

"You okay, bud?" Cosimo's voice came to Roberto as if it was from underwater.

"I'm jusss tryin' shtand up so I c'n pee," Roberto replied, taking his time to annunciate each word carefully.

"You're already standing up."

Roberto looked down at his feet and frowned. "When that happen?" he asked.

"You've been standing for a few minutes now," Cosimo replied. Roberto focused on the bar again. It was still tilting. Roberto had an alarming thought.

"Did I already g'pee?" he asked.

"I hope not," Cosimo said.

"Bar's tilty."

Out of the corner of his eye, Roberto saw Cosimo shake his head.

"Okay, man, let's get you home," Cosimo said, standing up and putting an arm around Roberto's shoulders.

"I'm good," Roberto said. "I d'need any help."

"Sure you don't, buddy," Cosimo staggered a little under Roberto's weight as he guided him out of the bar.

"We need n'Uber," Roberto said, pulling out his phone. He couldn't quite remember how to use it. "S'not safe for drivin.'"

"We can walk," Cosimo said. Roberto frowned at him in confusion. Cosimo pointed across the street. "Our place is right there."

Roberto burst out laughing. "You prolly don' even have Uber. You don' even know what'n'Uber's?"

"I know what an Uber is," Cosimo replied. "You wanna help me out and move your feet a little here?"

Roberto, who thought he had been walking, looked down to discover that they were both still standing on the sidewalk in front of the bar.

"Where w'goin?" Roberto asked.

"Crosswalk. That way." Cosimo pointed with one hand.

"Ver' smart. No jay-walk'n. Les go."

CHAPTER 23

Opposite Sides of the Wall

ANNE

Anne was sitting up in bed, a glass of wine in one hand and a book in the other. She had spent the last twenty-four hours thinking about how much she wanted to fuck Roberto Bonino and what exactly to do about that fact. She hadn't reached any conclusions, so she had decided to distract herself with reading and alcohol.

It wasn't working.

After about half an hour, Anne finished her wine and set her book down. She leaned her head against the headboard and sighed. Roberto's bed was literally on the other side of this wall. A foot away. Nothing but wood and insulation separating their beds.

Growing up, Anne always took it for granted that he was so close. The wall was thick enough that they couldn't really hear one another, and they certainly couldn't talk through it. But most nights, one of them would knock on the wall to say goodnight, and the other would answer. Three quick knocks in a row. When they were in elementary school, they had tried to come up with a complicated system of knocks to communicate. Two quick knocks meant "Do you want to come over?" Three slow knocks meant "I can't today." But all of them had faded over time, except for the goodnight knocks.

When Anne and Roberto were seventeen, his family had moved to a house on Tindale Way, on the other side of town. It was only four blocks to the west, but after so many years living side by side, it had felt like a hundred miles. The new house was where she and Roberto had been that night when they watched X-Files in the basement and kissed in the cemetery. The night that Gabby and Tom got in the car accident.

It still made Anne ache to think of it. Losing Gabby and Tom had been like losing part of her own family. But there was another, different ache there, too. It filled her chest when she remembered the way that Roberto had seemed to get farther and farther away from her with every second after that awful phone call, until he was actually and truly gone.

He left within forty-eight hours of finding out about his parents. After he had hung up the phone in the cemetery, he had sat in silence, rejecting any of her attempts to comfort him. After a while, he'd looked up at her and simply said, "I need to go." She had tried walking with him, but he'd shaken his head wordlessly and strode away. So Anne had just stood in the moonlight, watching him walk back to his house to get into his car and drive to the hospital in Silver Falls.

He didn't answer his phone for days, and when Anne finally knocked on the door of the house, Cosimo answered and told her Roberto was gone. He'd loaded up his car and driven to Chicago. A few months later, Cosimo sold the house and moved back to the apartment above the restaurant, and the room on the other side of her bedroom wall remained empty.

Until roughly one week ago.

Anne slid down until she was lying flat on her back in bed. An image floated into her mind, one of Roberto hovering over her as she lay here. The image felt tinged with danger, like if she opened the door to it any further, she'd invite something in that would devour her whole.

Maya probably had some kind of Wiccan "calm your libido down" spell if Anne got desperate, but based on their phone conversation, Anne doubted that Maya would share it.

Anne slowly reached up and grasped the top of her headboard, still imagining Roberto there above her. In her mind, she intentionally kept Roberto fully clothed. But still, she could almost feel the weight of him, the heat of his body close to her. She wanted to wrap her legs around his waist, feel the heat of him, move against him.

She closed her eyes, then let her arms fall back down to her sides. She sighed.

It had literally been at least a year since she'd had sex with anyone. After Tinder was a failure, she had tried a more extensive online dating service, and was dating more regularly, but it almost always meant a two-hour drive to Silver Falls. There just weren't enough people in West Tindale, at least in the off-season. Sometimes she had some luck during the summer, when tourists flooded the bookstore and the nearby restaurants and bar. But like she'd told Roberto that night, Tinder was a terrible place for her, and there weren't that many other options. She'd felt so overwhelmed by her last round of internet dating that she'd decided to take a break, and that break had turned into a kind of long-term holding pattern.

If she actually wanted to follow The Plan and get married, she'd probably have to get back into the saddle again eventually, but for now, she'd just concentrate on getting through the next week with Roberto.

As Anne reached over to shut her nightstand light off, she heard muffled sounds on the other side of the wall. Roberto and Cosimo's voices came through, low and quiet. She couldn't make out the words, just the slow, musical pattern of conversation. She smiled to herself. After a few minutes, the talking stopped, and Anne closed her eyes.

She had just barely drifted off, when she was awoken by a sound. It took her a moment to get her bearings, but then she heard it again. Three short knocks, from Roberto's side of the wall. Anne grinned. She sat up and knocked back. "Good night," she whispered, still smiling.

CHAPTER 24

Post Drunk Distractions

ROBERTO

Roberto woke with a splitting headache. He could usually hold his liquor pretty well, but he hadn't been quite that drunk in a long time. When he finally managed to sit up, Cosimo popped his head into the room.

"Hey, buddy!" Cosimo said.

Roberto held his head.

"How ya feeling this morning?" Cosimo asked.

Roberto groaned. "Thanks for getting me home last night," he said. "Sorry I was a mess."

"Eh, it wasn't too hard. And Very Drunk Roberto is kind of fun."

"Did I do anything stupid?"

Cosimo thought for a moment.

"Oh no," Roberto said.

"Nah. You uh…you did say a few things about Anne Winslow…"

Roberto's stomach clenched. "Like…what?"

"Oh, something about her hair being like a mermaid's? You may have used the word 'dryad.' I don't remember details." Cosimo was smiling.

"Yeah, you can probably just…forget about that," Roberto said. He paused. "Did I say anything else?"

"I think I got the general gist of what you were saying about Anne. Don't worry, I won't tell a soul," Cosimo said, and disappeared down the hallway.

That whole day with Anne, Roberto had a hard time concentrating. They spent the day going over floor plans and figuring out table arrangements, and then she worked the bookstore register while he sketched blueprints at a table nearby. His drunk self was right about her hair being like a mermaid's. Or a dryad's. By the time the day was over, Roberto was cross-eyed with lust.

Upstairs, Roberto turned on the shower and turned the knob all the way to cold. No more lustful Anne thoughts. He had already jerked off about Anne, and it seemed like jerking off about her had the opposite effect of what he wanted. He wanted it to relieve his feelings, but it seemed like it just made the longing worse. He wanted to stop thinking of her that way altogether. He swore through five minutes of freezing water, but it didn't do any good. After he had stepped out of the shower and toweled himself off, Roberto threw shorts and a t-shirt on and began pacing around his room. He felt like his blood was on fire. He thought about texting Lily or Kai, but they'd probably just tell him to keep it in his pants or go for a run, and he didn't really want to do either of those things.

He sat on his bed and held his head in his hands.

Why is it so difficult to think about keeping it in your pants? he thought.

Because Anne Winslow was hot as hell. Because he'd wanted her from the moment he even understood what it meant to want someone. Because when she bit her lip, his chest felt so tight he thought he might collapse.

"Okay," Roberto said quietly to himself. "Next question: do you have to keep it in your pants?"

He started pacing again. He was back to the same question he had been contemplating in the hotel room. Maybe Anne would be into it? A casual fling. There were plenty of women in his life that he'd had sex with and then been friends with (or at least been friendly with) afterwards. If he and Anne could remain friends after kissing when they were seventeen, surely they could remain friends after hooking up?

But you didn't remain friends, Roberto thought. *You didn't talk for eight years and then you sort of became friends again only because you happened to be in town and because the two of you happened to be thrown together to do this insane renovation project.*

Roberto ran his hands through his hair in frustration. He needed to do something productive with this energy, something that didn't involve his cock in his hand. He thought about the demolition project downstairs, and weighed the risk of Anne being down there against the promise of a good distraction from his thoughts. Physical activity was always a good way to clear his head.

Roberto headed downstairs.

It took Roberto a moment to find the light switch. He stood looking at the wall he and Anne had just demolished, and then he pulled gloves, goggles, and a facemask on. He started gathering up piles of drywall. It was a simple task to focus on. Pick up drywall pieces from this part of the floor and put them in garbage bags. Sweep this area. Do the same thing in the next area. When he had mostly cleaned everything up, he got out a handsaw and walked to the edge of what was now a giant doorway between the two businesses. He began sawing at the remaining chunks of drywall, evening out the edges, trimming what needed to be trimmed. When that was done, he looked up and decided to start the same process on the ceiling. He leaned the handsaw on a nearby chair and went to get a stepladder, pulling off his gloves and goggles and mask as he walked, just to get a breather.

But he had been staring at the ceiling when he returned with the stepladder, and didn't realize how close he had been to the chair, because when he stumbled on a piece of plastic on the floor, his right shin was suddenly filled with a searing pain.

"Fuck!" Roberto yelled. He looked down and realized that he'd stumbled right into the saw. A dark bloom of blood had started and was already running down his leg. "Fuck!" Roberto yelled again. He looked around for something to press against it, and finally tore off his shirt and pressed it to his shin. He sat on the chair and glared at the handsaw which was now on the floor.

"Fuck you," he said to it.

"Roberto?"

He looked up. Anne was standing in the doorway at the foot of the stairs. She was wearing pajamas, and her hair was wet, like she had just gotten out of the shower. She was frowning at him in confusion. Then she noticed the blood on his leg, and the way he was holding his T-shirt to it.

"Oh my god," she said and stepped forward.

"It's fine," Roberto said.

Anne crouched in front of him. "What the hell happened?"

"I tripped into a handsaw?"

"Jesus Christ, Roberto," Anne said, staring at the

bloody t-shirt. "This looks bad. You should go to the clinic. I can text Dr. Zhao."

"I don't want to go to the clinic," Roberto growled. It was late and he hadn't seen Dr. Zhao since he got back to town, and he really didn't have the energy to deal with "catching up" on top of a giant wound. He could see Anne's jaw tighten. "I really don't think it's that bad," he said. "It just looks bad."

Anne looked up at him. "Will you let me take a look at it? At least?"

CHAPTER 25

First Aid

ANNE

When Roberto nodded, Anne stood up and walked behind the counter.

"Is grown-up Anne okay with blood?" Roberto called out. Anne had been on the squeamish side when they were younger.

"If I wasn't, I would have passed out by now," she replied, walking back towards him with the first aid kit in hand.

Anne was very aware of the fact that Roberto was not wearing a shirt as she opened up the first aid kit. He'd kept his shirt on since that first meeting, and if she thought he was nice to look at before, this was next level. He didn't quite have a six-pack, but he might as well be a stupid statue of a stupid Greek god anyway. Anne knelt in front of Roberto and glanced up.

Oh. Never mind. He definitely had a six-pack. Anne told herself to be professional, even though she wasn't sure if the phrase was applicable in this situation. She wasn't an actual nurse or doctor, but this seemed like an inappropriate time to be ogling Roberto's stomach.

She pulled out alcohol wipes, disinfectant, gauze, and bandages.

"I hope you know this is breaking the rules," she said.

"Huh?"

"The rules we made when you first got to town. This is rule four. 'Shirts stay on at all times.'"

"It's the one rule we talk the most about," Roberto said.

"Because you keep trying to break it."

"I figured a major injury would give me an exception."

"Okay," she said. "Let's take a look."

Roberto slowly pulled the t-shirt away. The cut on his shin wasn't bleeding quite as badly anymore, but his leg was still a mess.

"Right," Anne said. "Are you okay with me cleaning this up a little bit?"

Roberto looked at her and then nodded. She stood up. "I'm going to go get a wet cloth," she said. "I'll be right back."

She walked to the back room and took a deep breath while she ran a cleaning cloth under the cold water of the sink. "Calm down, Anne," she whispered to herself.

Even his calves were attractive. His *calves*. Anne had never before in her life been aware of a man's calves. It had never even occurred to her that calves could be attractive. But this was not the time to be admiring a man's calves. This was a time to provide first aid to someone in need. Thoughts of his calves (or abs) (or shoulders) had no place right now.

Anne walked back into the bookstore and knelt in front of Roberto again.

"Okay, here we go." Anne worked quietly for a few moments, aware of being inches away from his half-naked body, and trying very hard to not think about it.

"It's actually not too bad," she finally said. "It just looks dramatic as fuck."

"I've been told I'm the same."

Anne looked up at him and smiled. "That you're not that bad, you just look dramatic as fuck?"

"It's my whole Tinder profile."

Anne laughed, then opened up an alcohol wipe. "Okay, I'm sorry—this might sting."

"Do your worst, doc."

Anne looked at him for a moment. "I just want it to be very clear that I am doing this because you are actually injured and need actual help, and not because I'm a woman who needs to take care of a man or something dumb like that," Anne said. She dabbed his shin with the alcohol wipe.

"Another rom-com trope you need to subvert?" Roberto said, teeth gritted slightly.

"We do keep getting into those, don't we?"

Anne worked quietly for a few more moments, until the cut had been cleaned and covered with gauze. She wrapped Roberto's leg with a bandage, just to keep the gauze in place, then pulled her gloves off and stood up.

"You probably should see Dr. Zhao in the morning, anyway," she said. "Can you stand?"

"Only one way to find out," Roberto replied. Anne stood in front of him, ready to steady him if needed. When he was standing tall across from her, he smiled. Anne reached out and placed her hands on his bare arms.

"Okay?" she asked.

"Yeah," Roberto replied.

Neither of them moved. Anne was suddenly deeply aware of her hands on Roberto's skin, of his bare chest in front of her, of his eyes moving over her face. His skin was warm under her touch. Her gaze moved to his lips, to a small fleck of drywall dust that had settled there. She looked up at his eyes, and saw that they were burning with something she couldn't quite name. Anne slowly reached her hand up and ran her thumb along his bottom lip, wiping the bit of dust away. His eyes fell closed for a moment. Then he reached out and caught her wrist and stared at her.

"Anne," he said.

She wanted to kiss him. She absolutely, 100% wanted to kiss him. It was all she could think about, the desire to feel his lips on hers. The thought filled her with warmth, and her whole body buzzed with longing.

Before she could talk herself out of it, she stood up on her tiptoes, leaned in, and gently pressed her lips to his. She resisted the urge to sigh with the goodness of it, of finally being able to feel this. After a fraction of a second, she felt his lips responding gently. When she pulled away, they stared at one another for a moment.

Then Roberto crouched, threw his arms around her waist, and kissed her desperately. Anne moved her hands over his warm shoulders, through his hair, kissing him back with such force that she could barely catch her breath. Whatever thoughts she had before she kissed Roberto flew out of her head. There was only the feeling of his lips, his skin, his hands. She felt herself being lifted up and spun around, and soon her back was against the wall near the register. Roberto pressed his whole body against hers, and then he pulled away slightly to move his lips like sparks along her jaw, down her neck, across the tops of her breasts, before crashing against her mouth again.

Anne felt like she was being tossed into a coursing river, no time to think, just the strength of the water carrying her away. Roberto slid one of his legs between hers, and she moaned as she moved her hips, grinding against his thigh.

She had never wanted anyone this badly. He pressed hard against her as his hands moved over her waist and down her sides. She needed more of him. She opened her mouth and felt his tongue move against hers. She wrapped her arms around him and pulled him even closer to her.

** CRASH **

Anne and Roberto came apart. It took Anne a moment to reorient herself. She looked down. Tools were scattered everywhere, a box of screws opened and littered across the floor. In their passion, they had knocked a chair over, and everything that was sitting on it. She looked back up at Roberto.

He was breathing heavily, looking at her, his lips slightly red and swollen. Anne's eyes strayed down to the front of his shorts, to the hardness that was evident there. Roberto was looking down at the tools around them. Then he looked back up at her and let out a small, uncertain laugh.

Their kiss in the cemetery from years ago came rushing back to her. And now he was standing there, everything she'd ever wanted when she was seventeen, giving her something that she knew he was going to take away again in a week.

He's going to ruin everything, Anne thought. Without a word, she walked past him and climbed the stairs to her room.

CHAPTER 26

Asking Advice

ROBERTO

Roberto stood in the empty bookstore, staring at the steps that led up to the Winslow's apartment. He reached a hand up to his lips. He could hardly believe what had just happened.

He didn't know that it would be like that. It hadn't even been like that when they were seventeen, that time in the cemetery. Granted, they had been young and didn't know exactly what they were doing, but still. Roberto realized he was still breathing heavily. His arms felt empty, and he knew that for the rest of his life, no shower jerk-off session would ever be as good as kissing Anne Winslow against this wall had just been. His injured leg didn't even hurt anymore.

Roberto turned and walked back through the hole in the wall. He marched upstairs and fell onto his bed.

She had kissed him first. All this time, he could have done it, and she probably would have kissed him back.

But then she had turned around and walked away without a *word* and he had no idea what it meant. It was late, but he reached for his phone anyway.

When Lily answered, he said, "I'm going to do something I've never done in my life."

"Okay," Lily replied with a question in her voice.

"I need your advice."

"Oh holy fuck, you really have never done that."

"I know, but I'm losing my shit and I don't know what to fucking do."

"I know it's a small town, but seriously, Bonino, you'll survive."

"That's not what I'm talking about."

Lily was quiet on the other end of the line. Roberto took a deep breath, then lowered his voice. Anne was probably right on the other side of the wall. "Hold on, lemme go outside."

When he'd made it to the back door downstairs, he spoke again. "I made out with my best friend from high school and then she walked out of the room without saying *anything* and my chest feels weird and I have no idea what's going on."

"Oh," Lily replied. She seemed to take a moment to process all this. Roberto had never really told Lily much about his life in West Tindale. And he had never told her about Anne. It was part of Chapter One of his life, and Chicago was Chapter Two. He'd put a hard line of separation between the two chapters. Lily knew he grew up in a small town in Montana and that his parents were dead, and that was it. His unwillingness to tell her more was probably one of the reasons they'd drifted apart when they were dating.

"Okay," she finally said. "Clarifying question. Do you mean you guys were going at it and then she just stood up and left?"

"We sort of got interrupted. We knocked over a thing

of tools and then she just stood there and looked at me and then she walked away."

"Knocked over a thing of tools, huh? That must have been some make out."

Roberto closed his eyes. "Yeah," he said.

"Okay. So. What do you want to do?"

"I mean, honestly?"

"Honestly."

Roberto sighed. "Honestly, I want to fuck her brains out."

"That feels like a short-term answer."

"It is."

"Do you want to fuck her brains out long-term?"

Roberto was quiet while he thought about this. "I don't know. I think the more important question is whether or not she wants to fuck *my* brains out long-term."

"Fair. Keep going."

Roberto closed his eyes. Lily had always been good at talking him through things. "She's got this plan," he said. "This life plan she's had since she was like, fourteen. Go to college in New York City, come back to West Tindale and marry a nice boy and live in a cabin and help her mom with the family bookstore."

"And you don't want to live in a cabin in West Tindale," Lily added.

"Right."

Lily sighed in sympathy. "Well," she said. "What would you usually do in this situation?"

"I've never been in this situation," Roberto replied.

"I mean if you made out with some girl here in Chicago and she was like 'I wanna live with a boy in a cabin in the woods.' What would you do?"

"Honestly, probably just ghost her."

"Okay, not the most mature response but we can put that down as an option."

"Yeah, it's not really an option. We're working together on the renovation."

"Well, shit."

"'Well, shit' is right."

"Okay," Lily said. "Actual option one is that you completely bail and get on a plane and come back home and never speak to this girl ever again."

"I can see both pros and cons to this plan," Roberto replied. "Pros include I don't have to deal with it. Cons include I might never be able to speak to my brother again?"

"Also, you're there doing your version of rehab, and it would suck to bail. So not the greatest option. Option two is that you pretend it didn't happen and just go about your life and basically forget about it."

"Also pros and cons, but I'm more concerned about whether or not that's even possible."

"Fair. Option three—wait, hold on, Kai just came home. Can I put you on speaker?"

"Yes."

"Hey, babe!" Lily called. "Roberto made out with this girl he's working with and he wants to fuck her brains out but she wants to marry a nice boy and stay in West Tindale. *He called to ask for advice.*"

"Whoa, Roberto Bonino is asking for advice?" Kai's voice got louder as he approached the phone.

"Fuck off, Kai," Roberto replied, loud enough to make sure Kai could hear him.

"So why can't you fuck her brains out?"

Roberto sighed. "Because I don't fucking want to stay in West Tindale."

"This isn't the 1950s," Kai said.

"I know, it just feels like the situation is more complicated than that," Roberto said.

"Bruh, you don't have to marry her," Kai replied.

Roberto was quiet.

"Oh, shiiiiittttt," Kai said. "Are you catching feelings?! Is our boy catching fucking feelings?!"

"It's not that," Roberto said, although he was afraid that it might be that.

"Why else would it be complicated?" Kai asked.

"There's just a lot of fucking history there, man!" Roberto replied.

"How long have you known this girl?"

"Since kindergarten? Before that? Our whole lives?"

Lily chimed back in. "You didn't tell me that!"

"I didn't think about it," Roberto replied. "Everyone has known each other their whole lives in West Tindale."

"Okay," Lily said. "I know this is going to be controversial, but have you thought about just…you know…talking to her?"

"What would I even say?"

"You could try something like 'Hey, just checking in'?" Lily suggested. "'Do you want to talk about what happened'? Or 'Hey, that was fun, do you want to do it again'?"

"But what if she says no?" Roberto asked. He felt like a little kid as he asked it.

"To which question?" Lily said.

Roberto thought. "Any of them."

"So she says no," Lily said. "If she doesn't want to talk about it, then problem solved, you don't talk about it and you just have to deal. If she doesn't want to do it again, then you deal with that, too. You've never had a problem getting pussy before."

Kai chimed in again. "Seriously, bruh, Lily's right. You can deal no matter what this girl says."

"If I wasn't monogamous as hell," Roberto said, "I'd ask to marry both of you."

Lily and Kai both laughed. "And I'd say no," Lily replied. "But I'm sure Kai would be down."

"Hella down," Kai said.

CHAPTER 27

About Last Night

ANNE

Anne slept terribly. For one thing, she heard Roberto talking on the other side of her thick bedroom wall for a few minutes, although she couldn't hear what he was saying. He had walked out of the room, the low rumble of his voice fading until she couldn't hear it anymore. Anne laid in bed, replaying their kiss in her mind over and over again.

Their kisses? Plural? That was definitely more than "a kiss." She kept tumbling headfirst into feeling like everything had shifted. Like there was a world pre-kiss and a world post-kiss, and now she was in a new place and felt a little disoriented. It had been the same way when she was seventeen, but the post-kiss world back then had been filled with so many other important things that she hadn't even had time to process. Now, she couldn't think about anything else. Just as she was finally falling asleep, towards dawn, she was awoken by a scream from downstairs. She sat up in bed.

"Mom?" she called out.

"Annie! Annie, what the hell?!"

"Mom, what is it?" Anne stood up and threw on a pair of sweats. Her mom met her when she was halfway down the stairs.

"What the hell happened last night?"

Anne's mind flashed back to having her back against the wall, Roberto's hips pressed against her, his lips moving with hers.

"What do you mean?"

"Why is there a fucking bloody t-shirt and a mess of tools downstairs?!"

"Oh my god," Anne said, her hand flying to her mouth. "Roberto cut his leg on a hand saw while he was working on the wall last night."

"Good Gaia, is he all right? That's a lot of blood," Debbie asked. "Did he see Dr. Zhao?"

Anne shook her head. "No, I bandaged him up and then…and then went to bed."

"Well, the clinic was closed last night anyway. Are you okay?"

Anne felt herself blush and turned around to go back upstairs. "Yep."

"Angels and ministers of grace defend us. Get dressed and come help me clean this up."

Anne did not see, speak to, or text Roberto Bonino for the entire morning. After she and Debbie cleaned up the tools (and blood) from last night, Anne stood at the book-store register and tried to not think about him and failed miserably.

She hadn't kissed an enormous amount of people—maybe a dozen or so—but none of them had ever kissed her like that. Anne couldn't figure out if it was technique or their history together, but either way, it was some next-level making out, and Anne wanted more of it.

Maybe?

Maya was going to lose her mind when she found out. Although Anne wasn't quite sure if she wanted to tell her. Maybe because she knew that Maya would ask "Okay, so what now?" and Anne didn't have an answer for her.

She was going to have to talk to Roberto again eventually. She was probably going to have to talk to Roberto again *today*. She was feeling vaguely panicked at the thought when he walked into the room.

Roberto looked at her for a moment, but before either of them could say anything, he was waylaid by Debbie, who had been straightening shelves nearby.

"Oh my god, Roberto!" she said. "Anne told me about last night!"

Roberto shot Anne a panicked look, and Debbie grabbed his arms. "Is your leg okay? Have you seen Dr. Zhao?"

Roberto looked visibly relieved, which he then tried to hide. "My leg is okay," he said. "Doesn't even hurt this morning." His eyes flickered back up to Anne, but soon Debbie was steering him to one of the tables and forcing him to sit down.

"Well, you rest here," she said. "I've got some things that will help. Don't move, I'll be right back." Debbie walked up the stairs, and Roberto and Anne were left alone. She avoided looking at him for a few moments, and then finally met his eyes.

"Hey," she said.

"Hey," he replied.

They were both quiet again.

"So I was—" Anne started, right as Roberto said, "I was thinking—"

They stopped.

"Sorry, what were you going to say?" Roberto asked.

"Oh. Um. I was thinking. Uh. Should we…talk? About last night?"

Roberto searched her face for a moment, then shrugged. "Not if you don't want to," he said. "We're cool in my book."

Anne was taken aback for a moment, and then found it in herself to nod. "Okay." *"Cool in my book,"* she thought to herself. *I guess that answers that.* She was surprised at how much her stomach dropped. She wanted to ask what exactly was on his mind, why he had kissed her like that, how long had he wanted to, did he want her as much as she wanted him, what did it all mean? But she swallowed it all down. "What were you going to say?" she asked.

"I was going to ask if we should hand out some flyers for the restaurant at the Fall Festival tomorrow. About the café bookstore launch. Cosimo had the idea. He wants to get the word out as much as possible."

"Oh. Yeah. That's a great idea. I'll draw some up this afternoon."

Another silence crackled between them. Anne's eyes moved to Roberto's lips…lips she had kissed just a few hours before. She wondered if he was thinking about it, too. She resisted physically shaking her head to snap herself out of her thoughts.

"Do you need any construction help today?" she asked.

"Nah, I should be fine."

Debbie came back down the stairs. "Okay," she said. "I know you don't believe in this stuff, but it really works. This is tea tree oil, and this crystal is called selenite…"

Roberto smiled up at Anne. "I'll take whatever you've got, Debbie," he said. "Anne fixed me up with some tradi-tional Western medicine last night, so now I need the other stuff."

"I've always believed there's great value in both,"

Debbie said, kneeling in front of Roberto. "Some people think they're opposites, traditional and magical remedies, but it's really more that they work in tandem with one another."

Roberto looked over at Anne and gave her a small smile, and Anne felt it in her core.

CHAPTER 28

The Fall Festival

ROBERTO

Roberto hadn't been to a West Tindale Fall Festival since he was maybe thirteen. At fourteen, he had decided that the local celebration was "dumb" and had preferred to stay at home and play video games with friends, which, in hindsight, wasn't any more or less dumb than a block party with food and music and face painting. The festival had been going on for at least thirty years. Back in the 80s, a few parents had gotten up in arms about the "satanic nature" of Halloween, so the city put on the not-strictly-Halloween fall festival every year instead.

When Roberto walked into the bookstore to meet Anne, she greeted him in a flow-y off-white peasant blouse and a laced-up, corset-looking dress that he couldn't quite figure out, but sure liked the look of. The memory of their kiss came rushing back to him, a heat in his groin and chest. He blinked the thought away as quickly as he could.

"You look festive," he said.

"Just wait," Anne replied, smiling. She pulled out a delicate flower crown and placed it on her head. The plastic and fabric blooms nestled into her red hair and something about it brought out the green of her eyes. Roberto's chest tightened, and he resisted the urge to place a hand over his heart. Then he looked down at his sweatshirt and jeans.

"Should I have dressed up?" he asked.

"No," Anne said, walking to the bookstore register to grab a stack of flyers. "I'm just extra."

"Either that or the rest of us are all basic," he replied.

"If you get desperate, you can get your face painted," she said, handing him half of the flyers.

The Fall Festival took place in the city park, just a few blocks away, so they sauntered easily down the street. Roberto and Anne planned to drop a stack of flyers with every merchant, post a few where they could, and then hand out the rest as they wandered.

"Hey, do they still do that fry bread?" Roberto asked.

"Dude. The day they stop doing that fry bread is the day I…eat my hat."

Roberto laughed. "I don't think anyone has said that since like, the Victorian era."

Anne smiled. "And I'm not even wearing a hat."

"The day you eat your flower crown."

"Exactly."

"Well," Roberto said. "I vote we go there first."

Without even thinking about it, he started to reach his hand out to hold hers. He remembered just in time that they were just friends and not the kind who held hands. He put his hand in his pocket instead. Anne didn't seem to notice.

They could hear music as they approached the park. That carnival smell of frying oil and popcorn and cotton candy hung in the air. They stepped through the arch at the entrance of the park and made their way to the food section. They walked past booths selling arts and crafts, local businesses handing out flyers and lollipops, even a few old-school carnival games.

"This is fucking quaint as hell," Roberto said.

Anne looked at him. "Is that an insult?" she asked.

"No," Roberto said. "I just…forgot about it all."

Anne smiled at him, then tilted her head. "Is this another rom-com trope?" she asked. "The fall carnival?"

"Oh nooooo," Roberto said, then laughed.

"We already checked the hotel room one off, and the 'playing nurse' one."

"This makes it an even three."

Roberto liked this. He liked that he and Anne could joke about it. It would have been worse somehow if they didn't acknowledge any of it. It made him feel like he could breathe a little easier.

After they had each eaten three and a half pieces of fry bread (they split the last one), Roberto turned to Anne.

"Should we pass out these flyers?" he said.

Anne looked at him and licked honey butter off of one of her fingers, and Roberto was temporarily hypnotized.

"Whoa," he said.

"What?" Anne asked, looking confused.

Roberto hadn't realized that he'd spoken aloud, and had to scramble a little to explain himself. "Miss Winslow, you're trying to seduce me."

Anne laughed. "If I knew I could seduce men by just eating fry bread with honey butter, I'd be married by now." She wiped her hands on a napkin and stood up. "Yes, let's pass out these flyers." She gave him a wicked grin. "Unless you want to watch me lick honey butter off my fingers some more."

Roberto felt Anne's words rush from the tip of his toes to the top of his head. He stood up. "If I didn't know any better, I'd think you were flirting with me. Let's pass out these flyers."

Before they could go, though, a voice called out. "Robbie Bonino, is that you?!"

Roberto looked around, then his eyes widened in surprise. "Hi, Mrs. Carrusco," he said. A short woman with white curly hair was making her way towards them. Somehow, in planning to come to this festival, it hadn't occurred to him that he would see other people he used to know in West Tindale. But of course some of them would still be here, including the teachers he'd had when he was in high school.

"Good heavens, it's been years!" the woman said. "Come here!" She reached up and wrapped her arms around Roberto, then pulled away to beam at him. "Your brother said you're out in Chicago now, is that right?"

"Yep," Roberto replied. He was still trying to get his bearings a little bit. "And you're still teaching math?"

"Oh, sweetheart, I'm going to teach math until the day I die," Mrs. Carrusco replied. "They keep trying to get me to retire but I refuse. Oh, it's so good to see you, Robbie. How long are you here for?"

"Just a quick visit," Roberto replied. "I'm heading back in about a week."

"How lovely!" She turned to Anne. "How's the bookstore doing, Annie?"

"We're actually doing a big renovation," Anne said, handing the woman a flyer. "We're joining forces with Bonino's Family Restaurant for a bookstore café. We're planning to open 'Pages and Pasta' in the early spring. But we're both still open in the meantime."

"Oh, that's wonderful!" Mrs. Carrusco said. "We always knew your families would join forces one day," she added with a wink. "All of us teachers knew you two would end up together."

"Oh, we're—" Roberto started, but Anne cut him off.

"Well, we've got to pass out more of these flyers, Mrs. Carrusco," she said. "It was good to see you!"

"Good to see you, too," Mrs. Carrusco said. "And Robbie, tell Cosimo we'd like to have you two to dinner before you leave."

"Will do," Roberto said, turning and waving over his shoulder as he and Anne walked towards the other booths. He felt a strange twinge in his stomach. He hadn't thought about Mrs. Carrusco, or anyone else from high school, since he'd moved away. It was jarring to see her again.

CHAPTER 29

Leaving the Festival

ANNE

Anne separated out a stack of flyers to pass out to the next booth. When she glanced over at Roberto, he was frowning as they walked, his eyes on the ground. It made her want to pull him aside and kiss him until his frown was gone, but she knew that wasn't an option. (Even though the thought of it made her entire body tingle.)

"It was bound to happen eventually," Anne said quietly. Roberto looked up at her. "The town is one square mile, and you lived here for most of your life. Of course you were going to run into someone who used to know you." Anne intentionally did not mention that Mrs. Carrusco had also seemed to think they were together.

"Yeah," Roberto said, looking back down at the ground.

Anne reached out and touched his arm very briefly. "Are you okay?"

Roberto nodded, but didn't say anything.

At a booth selling fly fishing lures, a man from the library exclaimed in surprise at seeing Roberto and shook his hand vigorously. Roberto had smiled and answered

Kenny's questions, but Anne could see how tight his jaw was.

They were down to some of the last booths, their stack of flyers dwindling, when someone caught Roberto's arm. Roberto turned and his eyes widened. An older woman with black and gray curls looked at his face and her hand flew to her mouth. Tears filled her eyes. "Eugenie told me you were back in town! Oh, Robbie, it's been so long!"

"Maria," Roberto said simply, before she engulfed him in her arms.

It had taken Anne a moment to place the woman's face, but suddenly it flooded back to her. Zia Maria. The woman that helped the Bonino family when Roberto and Cosimo were small. She had moved to Silver Falls after a few years, but Anne knew she and Cosimo had exchanged Christmas cards every year since.

Anne looked at Roberto, who was hugging Maria a little stiffly, a blank expression on his face. Maria let Roberto go and wiped tears away. She looked at him and took her face in his hands. "Bambino mio, you've grown up so well," she said softly. "I'm so proud of you boys. I think of Tom and Gabby every day. I loved your mama like a sister, and I know she'd be proud of you, too."

Anne watched as Roberto blinked rapidly, his jaw tighter than ever. He simply nodded.

"Come," Maria said. "Come sit with me and tell me everything."

Roberto suddenly looked like a trapped animal. Anne reached out and touched Maria's arm.

"And Annie!" Maria said. "Oh, sweet girl, it's so good to see you, too!" Maria turned to her and hugged her tightly. When Anne pulled away, she smiled warmly.

"Thanks, Maria," Anne said. She glanced at Roberto, who was standing and staring at the ground. "And I'm so sorry, but Roberto and I actually have to get back to the restaurant and bookstore. The businesses are merging and we've got to go over some of the plans."

"You're merging?" Maria asked.

Anne smiled and handed Maria a flyer. "We're turning Winslow Books and Bonino's Family Restaurant into 'Pages and Pasta.' If you're still in town tomorrow, I'm sure my mom would love to say hi."

"I'm heading back to Silver Falls tonight, but I'm so glad I ran into you two." Maria stepped forward and hugged Roberto again, whispering something Anne couldn't quite hear into his ear. Maria was teary-eyed again when she stepped away. She cupped Roberto's face in her hands before placing both hands on her heart.

Roberto and Anne said their goodbyes, and then Anne started walking towards the exit of the park. Roberto didn't say anything until they reached the bookstore. Anne unlocked the door and flipped on the lights. Roberto came and stood inside for a moment.

"Thanks," he said quietly.

"No problem," Anne said.

"Where's Debbie?"

"She's still at the Festival. The bookstore has a booth," Anne replied.

"Oh, yeah," Roberto said, his eyes focused somewhere in the distance.

Anne looked at him. "Stay here a minute. I really do want to go over some plans. But I also want to get myself out of this." She gestured down to her outfit. Roberto met her eyes and she had a brief moment of imagining his hands on her waist, pulling the strings of the corset loose, lifting the dress over her head…

"I'll be right back," she said.

Up in her room, she threw on a simple sun dress. She

didn't feel like having her breathing constricted by her festival outfit, but a dress still felt right. She laid the flower crown on her desk and walked back downstairs.

Roberto was sitting in one of the chairs at a small table, looking a little more relaxed. He had taken his sweatshirt off and was wearing an old t-shirt she recognized as Cosimo's. She smiled.

"You've only been here a week and you're already stealing your brother's clothes," she said. Roberto looked up at her, then down at his shirt.

"It was probably my shirt to begin with," he finally said. "Cosimo stole it from me." He ran a hand through his hair and sighed. "You wanted to meet about something?"

Anne came and sat at the table with him.

"Yes, but it's not urgent. I mostly wanted to give you an out from the festival if you wanted it. I just had a question about furniture against one wall, but we can talk tomorrow if you want."

Roberto met her eyes and didn't look away.

CHAPTER 30

This One's Mine

ROBERTO

Even after she had changed out of that incredible corset-looking outfit, Anne was still stunning. Her hair fell in curls around her face, her dress hugging her hips. The way she was sitting pressed her breasts together, and the sight of her cleavage was driving him insane. But her eyes were even more mesmerizing. He realized that he was staring, but couldn't quite get himself to look away.

Finally, Anne raised her eyebrows. "Are you okay?" she said.

Suddenly the whole night flooded back into Roberto's chest. He put his elbows on the table and rested his head in his hands for a moment.

He somehow hadn't thought about the fact that there would be other people in town who would recognize him. He hadn't really gone anywhere in West Tindale since he'd been back. But of course Mrs. Carrusco was still here, teaching math. Of course the man from the library was still here. If he really thought about it, he was surprised he hadn't run into Tyler or Sean or any of his old classmates.

Some strange part of his brain had just assumed that because he left, everyone else had, too.

But he hadn't expected Maria. He hadn't thought about Maria in years, and even if he had, he didn't expect her to be in West Tindale.

Roberto had the alarming sensation of being thrown back in time. Back to a time when he hadn't run away, a time when he knew what he wanted for his life.

A time when he had parents.

He was back in Chapter One again. Seeing Maria had filled with an ache so deep he thought he might drown in it.

"Roberto?" Anne's quiet voice brought him back to the present.

He looked up. "I'm okay," he said. "It's just weird being back here, you know."

Anne nodded. "I can only imagine," she said. She looked at him for a moment more, then stood up. "Let's chat about renovation stuff tomorrow." She reached her hands out to help him up, and even though he didn't need the help, he took her hands anyway. He took a deep breath to try and stop the ache he felt about being back.

"Shall I walk you home?" he asked, smiling.

Anne smiled back. "Please," she said.

He kept one of her hands in his as they walked towards the steps that led upstairs. His whole body hummed with electricity at the feeling of it.

When they reached the stairs (which only took about four seconds), she turned to him. "This one's mine," she said.

"I had a great time tonight," Roberto said.

"Me, too."

Roberto took another deep breath, still holding Anne's

hand. "I know that's my line here in this scene or whatever, but I do mean it. I really did have a great time with you."

"Same," Anne said. "It's…it's good to have you here." She looked at him, then stepped in and put her arms around him. He hugged her back, his hands resting on her back.

He had meant for the hug to be strictly platonic, but heat began to flood his chest, moving down to his groin. God, she felt good. Her breasts pressed against him, and she was so soft and warm in his arms. He didn't want to let her go, maybe ever. He thought that if he had to stop holding her, he might die.

Roberto felt her nestle into him slightly, turning her face towards his neck. He suppressed the shivers that ran through him. He took a deep breath, then tentatively moved one hand up her spine, his fingers brushing over the nape of her neck and into her hair, before he finally stopped and let his palm rest on the back of her head. Roberto felt Anne's breathing speed up, and it thrilled him. He had touched her with a question in his hands, and he felt Anne's answer in her breath. He wanted to feel more of what his touch did to her. He wanted her to know what she did to him. He drew his fingertips in a gentle line down the back of her neck again.

She made the tiniest noise of pleasure, a quick, quiet desperate kind of sigh. Then he felt her stand a little taller and press her lips to his neck. He closed his eyes at the heat of her mouth on his skin. Anne pulled away and looked at him, her hands drawing down his arms until she was holding both of his hands. He met her gaze. She looked at him with heat in her eyes, a question of her own smoldering underneath. She bit her lip, then took another few slow steps backwards. Roberto held onto her hands until she was out of reach. Finally, she turned and walked up the stairs.

~

ROBERTO STOOD for what was probably a solid three minutes, looking up the steps where Anne had walked.

She wanted him. He was pretty sure she wanted him.

And he sure as hell wanted her.

He took the steps two at a time.

He raised his fist to knock on Anne's door, but right before he could, she flung it open. Her hair was a little wild around her face, and she was breathing hard.

"Anne, I—"

She grabbed his shirt and pulled him into her room. She shut the door behind him and pushed him against it. Her hands roamed across his shoulders, down his arms. She pressed her palms against his chest, then slowly drew them down, her fingers brushing over his stomach, exploring his body over the cotton of his shirt. Roberto stifled a moan.

"Anne," he started again, his voice coming out hoarse this time.

She looked up at him. "Kiss me," she said. Her words raced through him, filling his body with heat. When he hesitated, she laid her hands over his, where they held her waist. "You can leave if you want to," she whispered. "But…I want you to kiss me."

Whatever reason or intelligence or logic Roberto had left flew out of his mind. He pulled Anne closer to him and pressed his lips to hers. Her mouth was warm, and she tasted like vanilla and honey, and he had the sensation of wanting to devour her whole.

She parted her lips and he began to kiss her harder, his

hands moving down her back. It was an oasis in the desert, a meal after starving, a gust of warmth after being out in the cold. It filled him with relief even while it filled him with electricity. After a few minutes, Anne took Roberto's wrists and moved his hands to her breasts. He groaned, her tits full in his palms. He'd wanted this for so long. He'd been trying not to stare at her tits all night, and now they were here in his hands. Roberto massaged them, and then held them gently, his thumbs brushing over her hardened nipples, feeling them through her clothes.

Anne's head fell back in pleasure, and Roberto took the opportunity to let his lips explore her neck, kissing down towards her breasts before returning to her lips again. He couldn't get enough of her. He kissed along her cheekbones and took one of her earlobes between his teeth. Anne moaned, and the sound of it made Roberto feel like he was in another dimension. He was getting harder by the minute.

He pulled away and looked at her with what he was sure was desperation. "Bed?" he gasped. When Anne nodded, he crouched and wrapped his arms around her, lifting her off her feet. She wrapped her legs around his waist as he walked them both to her bed. Roberto laid her on her back, watching her hair fall all around her on the pillow.

"God, you're gorgeous," he whispered.

Anne bit her lip as she smiled at him. She didn't answer, but pulled him down onto her, her legs hooked over his hips. His cock was already pressed insistently against the front of his pants, and the heat of Anne's body against him was torturous. Then Anne reached a hand down and gripped the hardness of him firmly over his clothes and he thought he might pass out.

"Jesus, Anne," he gritted out. She lifted herself onto

one elbow and pushed him over so that he was lying on his back. She sat up fully, and in one swift movement, she pulled her dress over her head, revealing a blue and black lace bra and black lace panties. Roberto let his eyes roam over her body for a moment, then he lifted his shirt off. Anne had seen him without a shirt before, but he loved the way she was looking at him now. Part wonder, part hunger.

"Come here," he said.

They kissed and kissed and kissed, hands everywhere at once, Anne's weight over him feeling more miraculous than anything he'd ever experienced. His hips ground up against her, making her gasp when his length pressed at the spot between her legs.

After what might have been an hour, or maybe five minutes, Anne sat up, straddling Roberto's thighs. She laid a hand over his stomach, then slipped her fingers into the waistband of his pants. She looked at the bulge in front of her and then back up at his face, running her fingers along the inside of his waistband. "I want to take these off," she said.

Roberto could only nod. Anne's fingers moved swiftly as she unbuttoned and unzipped his pants and pulled them down, moving to the edge of the bed. While she was still at his feet, she gazed back up at him and reached her hands up to grip the top of his boxer briefs, pausing for a moment and looking at his face. He reached down and put his hands over hers, looking her right in the eyes, then gently pushed on her hands to help her pull his briefs the rest of the way down.

His cock sprung out, and Anne's eyes never left it as she crawled up to kneel between his legs. She reached out a hand and wrapped it around his cock. She slowly pumped him once, twice.

"Roberto," she said.

Roberto thought he might actually die. He couldn't believe how good it felt, to have Anne there, his cock in her hand, his name on her lips. He reached up and pulled her onto him.

CHAPTER 31

Six in the Morning

ANNE

After all this time, all those moments of stealing glances at Roberto's shoulders, his chest, his mouth, Anne couldn't believe he was actually here, in her bed, his naked body under her hands. Roberto kissed her so deeply that she felt light-headed. His erection was pressing against her stomach, and his wide hands moved over every inch of her arms, her back, her neck, her hips. It was like he wanted to touch all of her at once, like he couldn't get enough of her.

She couldn't get enough of him either.

She sat up so that she was straddling him, and began grinding against his dick, her panties already soaked. But it wasn't enough. Anne wanted him closer. She wanted skin.

She lifted herself up and reached behind her to unclasp her bra, then let the straps fall from her shoulders. When she flung her bra onto the floor and looked back at Roberto, he was staring at her tits with his eyes wide.

"Jesus Christ, Annie," he said. He pushed himself up to a sitting position and circled her waist with one arm, Anne's legs still wrapped around him. He circled his tongue over her breast, and then pulled the nipple into his mouth. Anne felt heat spread through her core, flood the space between her legs. Roberto turned his attention to her other breast, and Anne became aware of how heavily she was breathing, of how she was rocking herself against him. But it didn't even occur to her to be self-conscious. It was just the two of them, in this moment, nothing and no one else in this room. Roberto took his lips away from her tits and looked up at her. She almost cried out in protest, but then he reached down and slid one finger between her legs, over her panties.

Anne gasped. Roberto's other arm was around her back, holding her in place, while he moved his finger up and down, up and down, in gentle lines from her clit to her entrance. Every few strokes, he would use his whole hand, putting a little more pressure, and then go back to one finger. Within a few minutes, Anne was practically writhing on his hand.

"So wet," Roberto whispered. He pulled his hand away and Anne thought she might lose her mind. But then he laid her back onto the bed and grabbed the waistline of her panties. He looked up at her and she nodded, and he slowly, so slowly, pulled them down and off. When he was at her feet, he turned and pressed a kiss to her inner ankle. Then her inner knee. Then her inner thigh. With every kiss, Anne's desperate sense of need intensified. She had to resist grabbing his head and burying it between her legs.

When he finally got to her pussy, his breath was hot against her skin. He pressed his lips to her folds, then opened his mouth onto her clit.

Anne arched her back at the wet heat of his tongue. She reached down and grabbed a handful of Roberto's hair. She hissed out a sound filled with both relief and longing. But then Roberto moved his tongue in circles over her clit, and Anne swore softly. He sucked gently on her, then moved back down to her entrance. She began to buck her hips against him as he licked her steadily. "Fuck, Roberto. God."

Roberto lifted his head and crawled back up towards her. "Anne, I...please, I want to be inside you," he whispered. There was a desperate edge to his voice, and his eyes were almost wild with longing.

"Condom?" Anne asked.

Roberto froze. "Oh my god. I don't have any. Do you…?"

Anne shook her head.

"Wait!" Roberto practically leapt off the bed and found his pants, pulling his wallet out of one of the pockets. He opened it and pulled out a foil package. "Oh, thank god."

"I can't believe you had that with you," Anne laughed.

"Thank god I did," Roberto laughed back, the desperation still not gone from his voice. Anne watched him open the packet and roll the condom on, then crawl back over her on the bed. She reached down and guided him to her opening. He pushed himself inside and they both groaned.

It was everything she wanted, everything her body had been crying out for. The feeling of him inside of her met some deep primal need, a longing she hadn't realized could be this strong.

He stayed still for a moment, filling her up, holding himself above her.

"Okay?" he whispered, his voice low and lustful.

"Yes," Anne whispered back. "Yes. More than okay. Yes."

Roberto groaned again, then began moving in and out of her, his breath coming hard and fast. Anne wanted more, her blood pumping through her veins with an intensity she didn't think she'd ever felt before. She threw her legs around his waist and met him thrust for thrust.

Their bodies were slick with sweat, and she reached up and moved Roberto's hair out of his eyes. He smiled at her, and then his forehead fell onto her shoulder as he moved with more intensity. She could feel her orgasm building, heat radiating from between her legs. She reached one hand down and rubbed her clit.

"Anne, I'm close," Roberto whispered.

Hearing his voice, low and gravelly and full of heat, sent her over the edge. Her climax came crashing over her, sending waves of pleasure through her. With a few more thrusts, Roberto came, then collapsed on top of her.

Anne woke to find Roberto's arms around her. It felt so good to feel him there, his body warm against her back. She smiled and curled into him, sighing. And then her eyes flew open.

Holy shit. She and Roberto Bonino had *sex*.

Good sex. Anne thought back to his finger moving over her pussy, his tongue between her legs, his mouth on her neck. It was better than she had even fantasized about.

And now he was in her bed and she was in his arms and she had no idea what time it was.

Shit. What time was it?! Anne sat up on her elbows, then reached over for her phone. It was six in the morning.

"Roberto?" she whispered. He slept soundly on. "Roberto?" She tried a little bit louder.

"Hmmm," Roberto replied.

"Roberto, we've got to get up." When she turned back to Roberto, he was blinking his eyes open. He saw her face and smiled.

"Good morning," he said.

"Yes, hello," Anne replied. "You've got to get out of here."

"Why, what time is it?"

"It's six."

Roberto settled back into the bed. "That's way too early. Come back here."

"I want to, but my mom gets up at six-fifteen, so you either have to head out now, or you have to explain to her why you're leaving my bedroom at this hour."

Roberto looked at her for a moment, then sat up and started gathering his clothing from the floor. Anne sat up and watched him, smiling at memories of last night. When Roberto was dressed, he turned back to her.

"Last night was fun," he said.

She cringed internally. *Fun.* It had felt like more than "fun." "Fun" didn't seem like the right word to describe Roberto's voice, low and desperate, as she touched him. It wasn't the right word for the pulsing ache she had felt, longing to feel him inside her.

"Yeah," Anne replied, pulling the sheets up to cover her bare chest. She paused. "Actually…um," Anne started. "What…was last night?"

Roberto paused, then shrugged, and it stung Anne to the very center. "Had to get it out of our systems, I guess," he said casually. "An old teenage thing that we had to get out of the way."

Anne struggled to gather her words. "And now it's out of the way."

"Exactly. This," he gestured vaguely at the space between them, "can't go anywhere anyway, so." He paused, then smiled at her mischievously. "Is this going to fuck up our working relationship, Annabelle?"

Anne looked at him, the stubble on his jaw, his hair

messy in the morning light, his lips giving her a crooked smile. His beautiful goddamn crooked smile. She wanted to sit up and kiss his entire stupid gorgeous face.

But she took a deep breath and shoved that desire down. "No, this won't fuck up our working relationship," she said. "We can keep it professional."

"Cool. Okay. I'll see you downstairs later." Roberto opened the door quietly, peeked out, then turned and waved before closing the door behind him.

"Cool," Anne whispered to herself.

CHAPTER 32

It Can't Go Anywhere Anyway

ROBERTO

Roberto snuck upstairs to his own room, grateful he still remembered which step squeaked if you stepped on it in the middle. He tiptoed past Cosimo's closed door, then climbed into his bed.

This can't go anywhere, anyway, he had said to her. And he was right. So why had it hurt to say it? He'd seen something flicker through Anne's eyes when he'd said it, and he'd made a joke right after. But he was just being honest. He was being realistic. He was going back to Chicago in a week and he wasn't sure they could keep sleeping together while also keeping it casual. And there was no way in hell Anne would want to give up her plan of staying in West Tindale and getting married.

Roberto felt a brief, bright ache as he thought of Anne in a wedding dress, smiling with her sparkling eyes at someone standing under a wooden arch.

He shook his head. Their lives were at least one full-time zone apart, and that was one time zone too many to make anything work. They wanted different things. *This can't go anywhere, anyway,* he repeated to himself.

He repeated the phrase as he showered and got dressed. He was about to walk back downstairs to meet with Anne, but he couldn't quite imagine sitting across from her and not kissing her. And he was also vaguely afraid that he'd do something stupid like tell her how long he'd thought about her, and that seemed like the exact opposite of what he should do. He needed to clear his head.

When he got downstairs, he found Cosimo in the kitchen of the restaurant. It occurred to him suddenly that maybe he should be helping with the family business while he was in town. He'd grown up helping in the restaurant every summer, waiting tables and washing dishes and chopping vegetables. When he left for Chicago, he hadn't even thought about the gap he'd be leaving behind at the restaurant. He hadn't thought about anything but getting away, escaping all the ache and hurt and helplessness he had felt at seventeen.

"Hey, uh…do you need any help down here?" Roberto said.

Cosimo looked up from the list he was writing. "Nah, I'm good. I've got a system. And it's usually slow this time of year anyway. I hire a couple of people to help out during the summer, but nowadays, I can handle it on my own. Besides, you're here to work on the renovation."

"Cool," Roberto said. They were both quiet for a moment.

"Hey," Roberto said, a little uncertain.

"Hey," Cosimo replied.

"I uh…I'm sorry you had to do all this yourself. All these years." Roberto felt like the words were scraping his insides on the way out.

Cosimo studied him for a moment.

"I should have…" Roberto stumbled onward, "You were young, too, and I…I'm just sorry."

Cosimo looked down at the list he was making, and a silence stretched out between them so long that Roberto was worried that Cosimo hadn't heard him.

Finally, Cosimo looked up again. "Thanks," he said. "It's okay."

Roberto nodded. After a few more moments, Cosimo added, "Was there…anything else?"

"Um. I was going to ask if I could borrow the car, but now I feel kind of weird," Roberto replied.

Cosimo laughed. "Keys are on my dresser."

After Roberto had climbed into the driver's seat, he pulled out his phone and texted Anne.

ROBERTO: Hey, I've got to run a few errands today. Catch up tomorrow?

She replied almost immediately, with a simple thumb's up.

Roberto started the car, and headed into the park.

People came from all over the world to visit Tindale National Park. For a long time, Roberto had taken it for granted that he lived right on its border. Growing up, he had spent so much time exploring its hiking trails and swimming in its rivers that some part of him had sort of believed that everyone in the world lived like this. He remembered being shocked when he got to Chicago. It had seemed so…flat. And geometric. Everything was rectangular.

But he had been grateful for the difference. He didn't want anything to remind him of West Tindale, or the park, or anything back home.

So it was strange that he had this impulse now—to dive headfirst into the place he'd been avoiding for almost a decade. But something inside of him pulled him towards the park, so he drove down Outpost Way, past the edge of town, past the park ranger shack, now empty for the season. He drove for miles until the forest was thicker, until he saw some of the first snow of the year on the sides of the road. He pulled into a small parking lot, a wooden sign marking the trailhead for Roger's Pass. He pulled on a jacket and re-laced his running shoes.

On the trail, he began jogging, and his footsteps beat out a steady rhythm to his thoughts. *It can't go anywhere anyway. It can't go anywhere anyway. It can't go anywhere anyway.*

And it wasn't just logistics. Roberto knew it wasn't just because Anne had "The Plan" and he didn't fit into it. It was that Anne also didn't fit into the life he had in Chicago…working long hours in the city, nights in a club somewhere. It was the polar opposite of Anne's vision. Of course there was a part of him deep down that loved the idea of a quiet life somewhere, but he didn't know how to be that person.

That night, the night of the cemetery and the kiss and Cosimo's phone call, he had felt something inside of him shatter. He hadn't known he was made of glass, but then he heard those words, "There's been an accident. Mom and Dad are dead." When he heard that, he broke into a million pieces. And everyone around him had been collateral damage. He'd swatted Anne's hand away when she reached out to comfort him. The shards he had broken into had cut everyone close to him, and he never wanted to do that again.

He never wanted to shatter, and he never wanted to cut.

So it meant forgetting the way Anne had swung the sledgehammer, forgetting that night in the hotel room in Silver Falls, talking for hours. It meant forgetting the soft heat of her kisses, the way her hair spread around her on the pillow as she laid underneath him. They would have a professional working relationship and then he would go back to Chicago and that would be that.

He had to keep running to keep the crushing feeling in his chest from devouring him whole. If he ran long enough and fast enough, he'd outrun it. He'd been outrunning everything for eight years, and it had worked so far.

CHAPTER 33

A Wrench in the Works

ANNE

That morning, after Roberto left, Anne lay in bed for a long time, thinking over what he'd said. "Fun." "Had to get it out of our systems." In the moment, last night, Anne hadn't thought about what any of the sex meant. She'd just been there with him. For Roberto, it was clearly a one-time thing, but Anne wasn't entirely sure what it had been for her.

The question tumbled around in Anne's mind as she got up, as she showered, as she sat behind the register at the bookstore. When Roberto texted her about running errands, she couldn't think of anything to reply with but a thumb's up.

Even despite her sense of disappointment that it was a one-time thing for Roberto, Anne spent the entire day getting delicious flashbacks of the night they had spent together. The way he'd called her gorgeous. The way he'd lifted her off her feet so easily. His voice when he'd whispered "I'm close." But when she wasn't smiling to herself about those memories, she was trying to get her bearings in their relationship. Maya always said that sex changes things. Even if you say it won't, it always does.

It seemed implied that she and Roberto would keep their night together a secret, but Anne also desperately needed some kind of outside perspective. She figured she could swear her best friend to secrecy. She texted Maya.

> ANNE: Emergency. Meet me for drinks tonight?

When Anne walked into the bar later that night, Maya was already sitting with a glass of white wine. Anne sat down beside her and ordered a glass of wine for herself and then looked over at Maya.

"So? Emergency?" Maya said.

Anne looked away for a moment, trying to figure out where to start.

"Oh my god," Maya said.

Anne turned to her in surprise. "What?"

"Oh my god, you fucked Roberto Bonino!"

"Not so loud!" Anne whispered back fiercely, but she couldn't hide her grin.

"Oh my god. Oh my GOD!"

"How the hell did you even guess that?" Anne said.

"Because I'm magical. And maybe it's because we've known each other forever, but I just looked at you and knew."

"Fine, yes. We had sex."

"Aaaaaannnnddd?"

"And it was very very very good."

Anne told Maya how she and Roberto had kissed a few days before, which caused Maya to hit her arm in mock fury for not saying anything earlier. Anne withheld details about the sex itself (most of them), despite Maya's begging for them. She ended with telling Maya what Roberto had said before he left that morning. About it just being a fun, "get it out of our systems" hook up.

"Ouch?" Maya said.

"Yeah," Anne replied. "Ouch."

"So. You finally finally finally had sex with your childhood best friend, and it was amazing, but probably a one-time thing, and now the emergency is 'how the hell do we get through the next week?'"

"Yeah. And also maybe just…help me figure out my brain. I don't know what to think or what to feel or if any of that even matters."

"Do you want a tarot reading?"

Anne shook her head. "Just…remind me why I can't fall hard," Anne replied.

"Why can't you fall hard?" Maya asked.

"Because he's leaving in a week," Anne said.

"Right," Maya said. She seemed to be lost in thought for a moment, then leaned on her hand and looked over at Anne. "But if he wasn't leaving in a week?"

Anne thought for a moment, then shook her head. "But he is. Hypotheticals will just…confuse me."

"Fair."

"So I guess…I just…forget about it?" Anne added. "Act like it never happened?"

Maya paused before answering. "Honestly, I don't know what other choice you have, babe."

"This is completely unfair," Anne said after a moment. "It's like the pilot light in my pussy is on even though the furnace isn't usable."

Maya laughed. "That sounds terrible," she said. She looked at Anne again. "Will you at least confirm or deny that as a Scorpio sun slash Taurus moon, he is good in bed?"

Anne smiled. "One time isn't quite enough times to confirm or deny, but…"

"But you're confirming it?"

Anne nodded, her smile widening.

When Anne got back to her room that night, she closed her door behind her and leaned against it, her eyes closed. When she opened them again, her gaze landed on the clothes she'd pulled off last night. The clothes that she and Roberto had pulled off her body.

Ugh.

Well, fine. If she couldn't have Roberto in her bed, then he could live in her thoughts. She climbed into bed and pulled her vibrator out of her nightstand drawer.

THE NEXT MORNING, Anne walked downstairs to find Debbie, Cosimo, and Roberto sitting at a table in the bookstore, having a serious discussion. For one panicked moment, Anne was afraid they were talking about her and Roberto, but as she got closer, she saw blueprints and notebook paper spread out on the table in front of them.

Roberto was wearing a button-up shirt with the sleeves rolled up over a t-shirt and jeans. What was it about a button-up shirt with the sleeves rolled up? That look always awoke some kind of primeval lust in Anne. She took a deep breath and glued what she hoped was a neutral expression onto her face.

"Hey," she said, joining them. "What's going on?"

"Nothing good," Debbie said. "We've got a problem. It turns out that we need to replace the columns and studs where the wall was, and there are also some issues with the electrical."

Anne made eye contact with Roberto, and he gave her

a small smile. "Maybe we shouldn't have knocked down the wall after all," he shrugged.

"So what does this mean?" Anne asked.

"It means we're delayed by a couple of months," Cosimo said. Anne met Roberto's eyes briefly.

"A couple of months?" she said.

"Roberto's agreed to stick around for longer—he's been able to work it out with his job back in Chicago," Cosimo said. "He'll be here for another month, instead of another week."

Anne's stomach dropped.

"But that's not even the biggest issue," Debbie said. She covered her face with her hands and leaned her elbows on the table. "We need an expert electrician to come in to help us meet the fire code. It sounds like the whole building —both sides of the building need to be completely rewired. And we don't have the budget for it."

Anne was quiet for a moment as she looked around the table. "How much do we not have the budget for it?"

Debbie looked at her. "We're already at our credit limit with the bank, and neither business has been successful enough to secure another loan anywhere else. So unless one of us can be approved for a personal credit card with a huge limit, we can't afford to finish this renovation. At all."

"We were just trying to figure out what to do when you came down," Roberto said.

Anne was still processing the revelation that Roberto would be around for another month, but she pushed the thought aside to focus on the budget issue.

She thought for a moment.

"What about a fundraiser?" she said. "What if we have some kind of event here at the bookstore?" Everyone at the table looked thoughtful. "Our poetry nights are always crowded," Anne continued. "We could have all the regulars, and Cosimo could cook, and we could even advertise in Silver Falls."

"Do you think we could raise enough?" Debbie asked.

"How much do we need?" Anne replied.

"The conservative estimate we were given was $15,000." Anne blinked. It was more than she had anticipated. But when she thought about how many people in their town loved their little bookstore, when she thought about the tourists who had been coming regularly every summer since she was a kid, it gave her a glimmer of hope.

"Okay then," she said. "Let's raise $15,000."

CHAPTER 34

We Just Decide

ROBERTO

They spent the next few hours brainstorming and planning. Anne brought her renovation notebook downstairs and added a section for the fundraiser. With her organizational skills at the helm, they soon had a name for the event ("Pages and Pasta Palooza"), and everyone had assignments. Anne would design posters and handle advertising outside of town, Debbie would handle decor and set up, Cosimo would handle food and advertising in town, and Roberto would help everyone out with whatever was needed, while still focusing on the details of the renovation itself.

Roberto had studiously avoided watching Anne too closely while they planned, and had suppressed a smile when she opened her notebook. He had felt a vague sense of panic at needing to maintain distance from Anne for another month, when they were going to be in such proximity, but he had sternly told himself to be an adult, and he was determined to succeed.

So when Anne suggested they drive to Silver Falls together the next day, Roberto agreed. It would take two of them to put up posters and advertise to schools and libraries and bookstores and cafés and anywhere else they could think of.

Roberto hadn't *intended* to throw himself into Anne's company again so thoroughly, but the trip to Silver Falls just made the most sense. He had to get supplies for construction, and Anne knew her way around the places they needed to go to advertise. The next morning, as he grabbed things from his room to prep for the drive, he told himself that spending the entire day with Anne would be a "baptism by fire" situation. Getting the worst over with as soon as possible. Like learning to drive a car with a stick shift before getting your first car with an automatic transmission.

When he climbed into the passenger side of Anne's car, she didn't make eye contact with him. "Ready?" she asked.

"Ready," he replied.

Roberto had expected some conversation on the two-hour drive, but Anne turned on a podcast and drove them out of town. The podcast was interesting, some history thing, but Roberto had a hard time concentrating.

He wanted to reach over and place his hand on the back of Anne's neck and run his fingers up into her hair. He wanted to take her hand in his. He wanted to rest his palm on her thigh. He wanted to tell her to pull the car over so he could tear her clothes off and make her moan his name.

He shook his head.

Just because you'll be here for another month doesn't mean you can keep fucking Anne Winslow, he thought to himself. *It was a one-time thing, and you got it out of your system, and now you've got to just keep this a professional working relationship.*

Besides, Anne hadn't even looked at him since…maybe yesterday? She had gotten into the car and turned on a podcast and ignored him. Even if he had the guts to make a move (which was a stupid idea anyway), he didn't know how Anne would react. It was a stressful project, coming up with a fundraiser in a matter of days, trying to raise $15,000 so that their family businesses would stay intact. Anne probably wasn't even thinking about him. She only threw walls up so that she could concentrate on the task at hand. Probably.

By THE TIME they'd distributed their posters, Roberto thought he could count on one hand the number of words Anne had spoken to him. If things had been chilly on the drive down to Silver Falls, they were positively arctic by the time they were driving back.

Anne had put another podcast on during the drive back, and at least twice Roberto had come close to switching it off and asking her what was going on. But he kept his hands firmly under his thighs.

When they finally arrived back at the bookstore, Anne got out and slammed the door of the car closed.

Roberto stepped out of the car and called after her. "Anne!"

"What?" She didn't turn around or stop walking. Roberto jogged to catch up with her.

"Anne, wait," he said.

She spun around and faced him, folding her arms. "What do you want?"

Roberto was quiet for a moment, unsure where to start. She raised her eyebrows at him. He half expected her to start tapping her foot impatiently.

"Are you…is this…are we okay?" he finally said.

"Sure," Anne said. "We're fine."

Roberto paused. "It doesn't seem like we're fine."

"I'm fine. I don't know about you."

Roberto weighed his options. He really, really didn't want to get into the nitty gritty of why Anne was being distant. But the thought of trying to just pretend like everything was fine when they couldn't avoid each other was worse. "If you don't want to talk about it, that's okay, but it just seems like there's something going on here." Roberto waited.

Anne stared at the ground. "I don't know, the fate of my family's livelihood is resting on one fundraising event taking place in a few days, during which we need to raise fifteen *thousand* dollars, or we lose everything. Forgive me if I'm a little tense."

Roberto was filled with the urge to take Anne in his arms, to rub her back and whisper to her about how it was going to be okay. He didn't know if it was actually going to be okay—fifteen thousand dollars was a lot of money for them—but it was difficult as hell to see Anne upset. He took a step towards her.

She hunched her shoulders slightly, folding her arms tighter. Roberto frowned. "Is that the only thing on your mind?" He held his breath, not even sure if he wanted to know the answer.

Anne was quiet for so long he wasn't sure if she had heard him. When she finally spoke, it was barely above a whisper. "I want us to be friends, but I don't know how. Maybe we fucked everything up."

Roberto shook his head. "I don't regret anything," he said.

"Me neither," Anne replied.

They looked at one another for a moment. Roberto spoke. "I think we can be friends."

"How?" Anne asked.

"We just…decide," Roberto said. "I'm deciding, right now, that we can be friends."

Anne studied him, and Roberto was temporarily distracted by her gaze. Her eyes really were truly stunning.

"Friends," she said.

"Friends."

"We just decide," Anne said. Roberto nodded.

Anne was quiet for a moment longer, then she unfolded her arms and strode purposefully towards him. When she was standing right in front of him, she held out her hand. "Okay," she said. "Friends." Roberto took her hand and shook it.

He knew he probably shouldn't have been turned on by the way she had walked towards him, but there was only so much he could control.

As he watched Anne turn and walk away, he had a sudden idea. He pulled out his phone and texted Lily.

ROBERTO: Hey can I get your help with something?

CHAPTER 35

Imaginings

ANNE

Anne wasn't sure what had come over her during her and Roberto's trip to Silver Falls. She'd felt furious all day, and it wasn't until Roberto asked her what was wrong that she realized her anger was covering a deep sense of terror. About both the bookstore and sleeping with Roberto.

The stakes really were that high when it came to the fundraiser. Until that morning, she hadn't fully processed what it would mean if they couldn't raise the money. She wasn't sure if they could keep operating the bookstore with a gaping, half-destroyed wall, and sales had been low anyway. And with the apartment above them, it meant that if they lost the business, they lost the place they lived as well.

But even beyond the practical worries, there were other reasons it would break her heart to lose the bookstore. So many of the limited memories Anne had of her father were of him standing in front of the shelves, or sitting in a chair with a book. Almost everything she knew or remembered of her dad was tied to the bookstore or the apartment above it. It had been his dream his whole life to run a bookstore, and it was part of the reason Anne had kept the bookstore in The Plan. It was her way of carrying on his legacy. She *wanted* to do it.

After she got inside, Anne waved to her mother behind the register and climbed the steps to her room. She collapsed backwards onto her bed and put her hands over her eyes. And on top of all of it, she still wanted to ride Roberto Bonino like a stallion. Which felt inappropriate given the circumstances. The fate of her late father's legacy and her family's livelihood was on the line, and still, Roberto just standing there, all handsome and sexy, asking her if she was okay…it made her feel weak in the knees.

But it also made her feel completely uncertain. She almost hadn't had time to really think about how she was going to manage the next month with Roberto around. She'd been so busy trying to figure out the logistics of a fundraiser, and then it was impossible to think about how to deal with Roberto when he was there in the car next to her.

Anne sighed. They were friends. They shook on it. Roberto seemed overly confident about their ability to just decide to be friends and then be fine, but if he could do it, maybe she could, too. There would probably always be a part of her that wanted Roberto—he was stupidly attractive—but that was manageable.

If they couldn't be together, then being friends was the next best thing.

Friends who had hooked up once. And also had kissed once, on a separate occasion. Well, technically, they'd kissed on two separate occasions, if she thought back to when they were seventeen.

Roberto said he didn't regret anything. The thought had flooded Anne with equal parts relief and fire.

She thought back to the way he'd slid his thigh between her legs, that night they'd kissed downstairs. The way she'd ground her hips with pleasure. She thought back to other times in her life when she'd been with other people, the sense of performance that was always there beneath the surface. With Roberto, there had been no self-conscious-ness or embarrassment. She'd just felt…safe.

Or maybe "safe" was too serene of a word for what she'd felt with Roberto. It wasn't a calm sort of feeling. But when she was with him, she hadn't felt embarrassed about what she'd wanted, or how she'd sounded, or how she'd looked. She just did what felt good.

"Free," she whispered to herself. That was a better word than safe. She'd felt free.

She remembered how he'd looked at her breasts in amazement when she took her bra off. He made her feel like a goddess. Something to be worshipped. She reached up now and held her breasts in her own hands. She ran her hands up and down her body a few times, over her clothes, exploring the divinity Roberto had seen in her. She closed her eyes in pleasure.

One of her hands reached down between her legs. She ran her fingers lightly over her sex, barely touching herself. She used one finger to draw gentle circles and lines over her clothes, running along her inner thighs, passing over her pussy, drawing up her belly.

She remembered taking Roberto in her hand in her bed, the velvet heat of his cock, the way it had twitched in her palm when she moved up and down its length.

Anne smiled and imagined sitting in the last row of a movie theatre, her hand resting on Roberto's thigh. She imagined leaning over, kissing his neck, watching his eyes fall closed as her hands undid his belt, unbuttoned his pants, pulled down his zipper. She imagined slipping her hand into Roberto's briefs, grasping his hardening dick.

She reached her hands into her panties.

He would reach up with one hand and run his fingertips over her breasts. Anne let out a small gasp at the thought. Her fingers moved over her wet pussy, with more pressure now. She imagined his lips against her ears, telling her how hot she was while she pumped his cock.

Anne rolled over onto her stomach and ground against her hand.

"You make me want to come, Anne," she imagined him whispering. *"Don't stop. God, that feels so good."*

Anne's fingers moved faster as her hips moved back and forth against her bed. She reached her other hand up and clutched the sheets. The pleasure was growing, the high note of a violin string resonating from her core.

"Roberto," she whispered. The image in her mind shifted, to a moment later in time in her fantasy, to Roberto's fingers moving expertly between her legs as they sat in the movie theatre. She imagined him reaching under her dress, moving her panties aside, moving his fingers faster as he whispered into her neck. *"Yes, baby, that's it. God, just like that. Come for me, Anne. I want you to come."*

In her bedroom, Anne's legs shook as her orgasm overtook her. She bit her pillow to keep from crying out. When her breathing finally slowed, she rolled over onto her back and sighed. She was asleep within minutes.

CHAPTER 36

The Fundraiser

ROBERTO

Debbie, Cosimo, Anne, and Roberto had spent the last three days working feverishly to prepare for "Pages and Pasta Palooza." There would be poetry readings and drinks, and Cosimo was making appetizers. Maya had come to drop off extra tables and chairs from the hotel. Roberto had snuck off to talk with Lily on the phone a few times a day, but he was pretty sure everything was in place for his plan to work. He was just waiting for the final word.

He really hoped it would all work, because the event was in an hour. He was in the bookstore with the others, helping them move shelves, set up chairs, and throw tablecloths over the extra tables. At the moment, though, he was watching Anne as she stood on her tiptoes on a step stool, ringlets of red hair falling out of the elaborate twist she had arranged her hair into. He came to when Cosimo punched his arm.

"Quit staring at Annie's ass," Cosimo whispered.

Roberto glared at him. "I wasn't," he whispered back, going back to his task of filling vases.

Cosimo just rolled his eyes. Roberto wondered how much Cosimo knew, or suspected, about him and Anne. He was debating the question when he felt a hand on his arm. He looked up to find Anne herself by his side, looking between him and the vases on the tables.

"Did you grab the extra baby's breath from the fridge?" she asked.

Roberto looked at her for a moment. She really was beautiful. It was the kind of beauty that would grow and shift and change as she got older...he could imagine her hair becoming white, wrinkles around her eyes. The thought made his chest ache.

"Roberto?"

"Huh?"

"Baby's breath?"

"Oh," Roberto replied. "Yeah, no. I didn't know we had any extra."

"I'll grab it," she said. Roberto watched her walk away, then realized that yes, he was staring at Annie's ass and he had better stop before Cosimo caught him. (Again.) He gave himself a mental shake and went back to filling vases.

Within a few hours, guests were arriving. Kenny from the library came and shook Roberto's hand. Mrs. Carrusco engulfed him in an enormous hug and rubbed his arms vigorously. Roberto had a subtle sense of claustrophobia again, but he thought of Lily's words from that text message a week ago, and so many other times before that. To just be in the room. This was for Cosimo, and Debbie, and Annie. He could stay in the room for them.

After his experience at the Fall Festival, Roberto was surprised at how many people he *didn't* recognize at the fundraiser event. There was a time when he would have known the names of everyone in the room in West Tindale, and maybe even where they all lived. But the town had been growing without him. There were familiar faces, but he couldn't put names to them, and there were still lots of people he couldn't place at all.

He did have a halting but friendly reunion with Tyler and Corinne, and it took him a full ten minutes to process it afterward. The first half of the night was just mingling, and even though Roberto could stay in the room for the people he loved, he couldn't quite bring himself to schmooze. He sat at a table and chatted with folks who came by, but mostly just watched everyone (and occasionally his phone). He was watching Anne chat with Maya at the moment, watching the way Anne threw her head back when she laughed, the way her eyes grew wide with excitement at something Maya said.

Cosimo came and sat next to Roberto. "If I didn't know any better, I'd think you had a thing for Annie Winslow."

"I've always had a thing for Annie Winslow." Roberto said it without even thinking.

Cosimo raised his eyebrows. Roberto wasn't sure what to say next. He hadn't planned on saying it...it had just come out. He didn't think he'd ever said it out loud. It was probably best to just change the subject.

"Where's *your* date for tonight?" Roberto asked.

Cosimo sighed. "Damned if I know."

"Wait, do you actually have a date tonight?"

"No. I was being sarcastic. There are no people to date in West Tindale."

"You're gonna die alone, old man," Roberto said.

"I know," Cosimo replied. "Debbie keeps trying to get me to marry Anne. But if anyone's gonna end up with Anne, it's you."

Roberto had no idea what to say to that. A significant part of him bubbled up with hope at the thought, while the other part of him sternly reminded him that nothing about it would actually work. But before he could come up with a reply for Cosimo, Debbie's voice rang out above the crowd. "Thank you all so much for coming! We——" Anne handed Debbie the microphone. "Oh, thank you, honey. We are all so grateful for your support. If you haven't already grabbed food, Cosimo's made some amazing appetizers over here for you to try, and in a few minutes, we have some local writers who have volunteered to share some of their work with us."

"Mom, remind them about the donations box," Anne said from the side of the stage.

"Oh yes! And if you'd like to make a donation to help us complete our renovation, you can put checks, cash, savings bonds, IOUs, spare change, jewelry, just anything you can afford in this big purple box up here. Our goal tonight is $15,000. We love being a part of this little community, and we are just so grateful you're willing to help us out even more than you already do. Have a wonderful night!"

Roberto smiled. He'd always loved Debbie. Beneath her flighty exterior was a heart that loved fiercely, even if she was always a little disorganized. Anne had probably learned to be so organized because she had to be, to make up for her mother's disorganization.

The guests went back to chatting, and Roberto's phone rang. Lily. His stomach flipped. He hit answer as he strode out the door into the cold.

CHAPTER 37
Upstairs

ANNE

Anne was sitting in her usual spot for Poetry Night, in a chair next to their makeshift "stage" area. The handful of "poets" and poetic hopefuls that often came to the bookstore's events had each shared something. Four-year-old Emily Young gave a reprise of her poem about trees. Kenny had come with a new piece about the park in autumn.

Hearing members of her community read poetry out loud was truly one of Anne's favorite things, but she found herself scanning the crowd for Roberto. He'd been disappearing off and on throughout the night. He'd met her eyes and put his hand over his heart when Emily performed her poem about trees, but slipped out again afterwards. Anne kept glancing around, checking to see if he'd come back yet. When he finally walked through the door and stepped into the back of the audience, Anne's heart made a small leap.

Calm down, heart, she said to herself. But she liked the way he stood, the way his clothes hugged his body. He was grinning widely, a giddy schoolboy excitement playing across his features. It stayed there as the next few people recited poems into the microphone.

When everyone was done, Debbie stood up at the microphone again. "Okay, friends," she said. "I just checked the donations box, and I want to thank you for the $8,000 you've raised for us so far tonight! We're still a little short of our $15,000 goal, so if you haven't donated yet, please drop your donations into the box before you leave!"

Suddenly, Roberto was at the front of the crowd, with his phone to his ear. He pulled the phone away briefly and said, "Hey, Debbie, can I make an announcement?"

Debbie looked at him, slightly bewildered, then gestured to the microphone.

"It's actually technically not me making the announcement," he said. "But I have the announcement guy on the phone." Roberto held the phone up to the microphone, then said, "Say something, Julio."

A voice crackled from the phone. It was a little distorted, but it was clear enough to be understood. "Can you all hear me?"

The crowd nodded, and a few "yes"es rang out.

"We can hear you, Julio," Roberto said, smiling.

"Okay," the voice said. "My name is Julio Jiménez, and I am the founder and CEO of Jiménez Building Design in Chicago. We were told about the fundraiser for your businesses, and as someone who started in a tiny office, I know how hard it is to grow. So our company has decided to match donations made to your cause tonight, up to $10,000."

Anne's stomach did a somersault. The crowd erupted into cheers. Debbie's hand flew to her mouth and tears filled her eyes. Cosimo had buried his face in his hands. Roberto was grinning.

Anne felt like her heart was going to burst. She made

eye contact with Roberto and for what felt like minutes, she couldn't look away. They'd met their goal. They'd met more than their goal. The business would work and they had a place to live and Roberto had helped make it happen. Anne's throat tightened, tears filled her eyes, and she turned and walked up the stairs to her room.

She made it as far as the upstairs landing before she leaned against the wall and covered her face with her hands. She was trying not to sob. She heard footsteps on the stairs behind her and hastily wiped her tears away.

"Hey," a voice said. She turned and saw Roberto looking at her with concern. Anne ran at him so hard that he stumbled slightly when she threw her arms around his waist. She buried her face in his chest.

"Hey," Roberto said again, more quietly this time, wrapping his arms around Anne. He was warm and solid.

"Thank you," Anne whispered. "I don't...I can't... thank you."

Roberto ran his hands up and down Anne's back. "It was no problem," he whispered back. Anne was filled with such warmth she barely knew what to do with it all. She turned her head slightly and planted a slow kiss on Roberto's chest.

"Thank you," she whispered. Roberto leaned his head against the top of her hair, then turned and pressed his lips to her temple.

"It really is Julio you can thank," he whispered back.

Anne lifted her head and looked at Roberto. She was aware that her face was tear-stained, and that her makeup was probably running, and that their embrace had probably squashed her hair. But the way Roberto was looking at her made her feel beautiful anyway. He reached down and cupped her face in his hands, gazing at her. Anne wasn't sure who leaned forward first, but suddenly Roberto's lips were pressed to hers.

The kiss moved through Anne's whole body. She moved her hands from his back, up to his chest. He moved one arm to circle her waist and pulled her into him, kissing her more deeply, and suddenly there was a desperation to their kisses. Her back arched, and his other hand moved down across her breasts, over her ribs, along her hips. Anne felt like she had so much emotion that there was nowhere else for it to go except into kissing Roberto.

Anne clutched his shirt, kissing him with everything in her body. When her fingers moved to the buttons near his collar, she heard him let out a small moan, a hungry sound from the back of his throat.

They stumbled into her room, closing the door behind them, locked into kisses so deep there wasn't even time to fully undress. They fell into the bed, and Anne pushed Roberto onto his back, then reached down and pulled her panties off from underneath her dress. Roberto had unbuckled his belt, unzipped his fly, and shoved his pants and briefs down by the time Anne knelt on either side of his hips. They were both breathing heavily, and Anne thought she'd never seen anything more beautiful in her life than this man, hair mussed, looking at her with unguarded desire. She looked into his eyes as she positioned herself above him, then reached down and guided his hardened cock to her opening.

She sank down slowly onto him, then leaned forward and put one hand next to his head as she began moving against his body. This was what she had been longing for, from the moment he had left her bed the last time. Words weren't enough to tell him how she felt, about him, about what he'd done for their families. Roberto's hands reached down and clutched her hips, then slid beneath her dress to grab handfuls of her ass. His eyes shut tight for a moment as she drove herself down onto his dick. "Annabelle," he whispered.

Anne leaned down and pressed her lips to his jaw, then she lifted her head again and looked at him. Roberto reached a hand up to hold one side of her face, then looked down at their bodies coming together again and again. When Roberto looked at Anne again, his mouth was open wide, his jaw pushed forward, his breath coming hard and fast, his eyebrows pinched together.

It had only been a few minutes, and Anne was already almost there. She sat up and placed her hands on Roberto's chest, moving faster. When her orgasm came, she clung to Roberto's arms, felt him holding her up as waves of pleasure radiated through her body. When the waves finally slowed, she fell weakly onto Roberto's body, his cock still hard inside of her.

"Annie," Roberto whispered. "Annie, please, I—"

Anne turned her face towards his ear. "I want you to come," she whispered back, then sat up so that she was still straddling him. "Come for me. Please."

Roberto sat up on one elbow and gripped the back of Annie's neck while he drove into her. He was looking at her in a way that no one had ever looked at her before, vulnerable and desperate, and when he came, he whispered her name through gritted teeth.

CHAPTER 38

Downstairs Again

ROBERTO

After a few moments, Anne slowly lifted herself off of Roberto and laid beside him, her head on his chest. They lay in silence, their breathing slowly coming back down to normal.

After a while, Anne finally lifted her head and looked at Roberto. "We should probably go back downstairs," she said. "Do I look like a mess?"

Roberto looked up at Anne, her hair frizzy, her lips red and over-kissed, and couldn't help smiling. "You look beautiful," he said.

Anne's smile started in her eyes and slowly spread across her whole face. She leaned down and kissed him softly. When she pulled away, she looked at him and reached a hand out to move his hair out of his face. She smiled for another moment, then climbed out of bed. A handful of tissues from her bedside took care of clean up. Roberto sat up and watched as Anne picked her panties up from the floor and stepped into them, pulling them up under her dress.

"We should probably not go downstairs at the same time," he said.

"Good point," Anne replied. "You go down first and I'll take a minute and put myself together again and come down after you."

Roberto stood and pulled his pants back up to his waist. He watched Anne as she adjusted her clothing, a small smile on her face. She looked up at him as he tucked his shirt in.

"Hurry up," she teased, grinning. "Quit standing there staring at how hot I am."

Roberto grinned back. When they were both fully dressed and put together again, Anne pushed him out the door, but grabbed his arm and pulled him back again to kiss him deeply. She held onto his collar and leaned her head against his chest.

"I didn't plan on having sex with you as like, a thank you for what you've done for the fundraiser," she said quietly. "But uh…thank you for what you've done for the fundraiser. Thank you, Roberto."

"You're welcome, Annabelle," Roberto replied, kissing the top of her head again. "I'll see you down there."

When Roberto got downstairs again, the room was buzzing with chatter. People were mingling and talking and laughing. Cosimo jogged over to him and grabbed his arm.

"There you are!" Cosimo said. "People have been looking all over for you. Where were you?"

"Uh…" Roberto glanced up the stairs behind him. "I was checking on Annie."

Cosimo studied him for a moment, then began dragging him across the room. "Okay, well, you need to talk to these people, because I'm going to die if I have to be in this crowd for one more second." With a final shove on

Roberto's back, Cosimo disappeared through the archway back to the restaurant.

Roberto spent the next hour shaking hands, explaining how he got the business in Chicago to donate, answering questions. Anne had come back downstairs a few minutes after he had, looking pretty and kissable. Between chatting with people from West Tindale and trying to not make it very obvious that he was watching Anne, he was exhausted within minutes. He wished he could follow Cosimo and escape to his own room.

Or to Anne's room again.

Okay, so maybe him and Anne sleeping together wasn't a one-time thing. Apparently it was a two-time thing. And if he was being honest, Roberto wanted it to be a many more times thing. They'd already shaken hands on their deal of being friends, but maybe…maybe they could be friends with benefits? Roberto really really liked the benefits. He had done the friends-with-benefits thing plenty of times before and it had been fine. Maybe this could be their summer fling. The one they didn't have when they were seventeen. Maybe it wasn't just sex they had to get out of their systems. Maybe it was a whole fling.

When the last guest had left, and Debbie had locked the door, she and Roberto and Anne stood and smiled at one another. Debbie walked over to the donation box and picked it up. "Where's Cosimo?" she asked.

"He was people-d out so he went upstairs," Roberto said.

"Okay, well you kids come with me."

Roberto and Anne followed Debbie to the back room. Anne reached out her hand and brushed her fingers briefly against Roberto's for just a moment, and Roberto had to concentrate on not getting hard or melting into a puddle.

Which was probably bad news for someone who just wanted to be friends with this woman.

Debbie opened the donation box and pulled the adding machine close to her. A few minutes later, she looked up with tears in her eyes. "There's almost $11,000 here," she said. "With the donation from your work in Chicago, that's almost $21,000." She stood up and put her arms around Roberto. She didn't say anything for a long, long time.

"For the rest of my life," she whispered, "I will never be able to thank you enough. Wherever Gabby and Tom are now, I swear I can feel them beaming at you for this. Love love love you."

Roberto hugged Debbie tightly and closed his eyes. "Love you, too, Debbie," he whispered.

CHAPTER 39
An Autumnal Fling
ANNE

Anne had been watching Roberto all night, desperate to have him alone again. It had been less than two hours since they'd been in her bedroom together, and all she knew was that she wanted more of it. Damn the consequences. She volunteered herself and Roberto to clean up downstairs and told Debbie to go to bed. It was partly because she could tell her mother was exhausted, but also because she wanted to talk to Roberto. Debbie fought them, but when Anne finally said they'd leave some things for her to do in the morning, she relented.

As soon as Debbie was out of sight, Anne looked briefly at Roberto and then started gathering vases of flowers from the tables. Now that she had him here, she wasn't quite sure what to say. Roberto grabbed the trash can and began walking from table to table to pick up napkins and cups.

Roberto spoke first. "Hey, so um…Anne?"

"Roberto?"

"I'm uh…about earlier…"

Anne's words rushed out of her mouth before she even

had time to think about them. "I don't know what's going to happen when you have to go back to Chicago. I don't know what any of this means. I just know that I like being around you. And I want you a lot, kind of all the time. So can I just have you for a little while? Just for now?" She was looking at the ground by the time she finished, and when she looked up again, Roberto was smiling at her.

"I would love for you to have me just for right now," he said, his grin widening.

Anne was flooded with relief and elation, and a little bit of…was it terror? She knew that what she was asking for was small and temporary. And she was terrified of what might happen afterwards, and how she'd feel after Roberto got on a plane and headed back to Chicago. But mostly she was glowing at the thought of spending the next few weeks with Roberto in her bed. Or in his bed. Or in her car. Or really anywhere.

"Just so we're on the same page," Anne said. "What I mean is sex. With you. You and me. Sex."

Roberto nodded. "No, yeah, I got that. That is the page I am also on."

"Good," Anne said, smiling at him. But then she frowned. She thought about her and Maya's conversation at the bar a few nights ago.

"Should we…tell people?" she asked. "That we're… kind of a thing?"

Roberto looked at the ground for a moment, then back up at her face. "Probably not," he said. "I'm not in the habit of announcing my sexual partners to the world, and I don't feel like trying to explain it all or dealing with everyone else's opinions or questions or anything. I just…want you."

"I wouldn't know how to explain it anyway," Anne replied.

"No one else needs to be a part of it. It's the summer fling we never had, just in November instead."

"So a secret autumnal fling," Anne said. Roberto grinned at her. "What?" she asked.

"Autumnal," he said, and strode towards her. He gathered her into his arms. "Say it again, baby," he whispered into her hair.

"Autumnal." Anne's giggles were soon lost in Roberto's kiss.

He pulled away a moment later and looked at her with a hint of concern. "We um…we didn't use a condom earlier tonight."

Anne startled. "We didn't," she replied. She had been so lost in the moment with Roberto that she hadn't even thought about it. She did some quick calculation in her head. "We should be okay, but I'll grab a morning-after pill just to be safe."

Roberto nodded.

"I'll also grab a large box of condoms," Anne added with a wink.

∼

A WEEK AND A HALF LATER, Anne pulled out her bullet journal, and opened to a clean page.

Locations Where Roberto Bonino and I Have Had Sex:
 1. My bed (x6)
 2. His bed (x2)
 3. My car
 4. The back room at the bookstore

> *5. On a blanket in the woods in Tindale National Park*
> *6. In the back row of a movie theatre (kinda)*

Anne smiled as she wrote the last one. They hadn't full-on fucked in the movie theatre, but jerking each other off in the dark was a great enough memory that it was worth recording. Afterward, she'd told him about how she'd fantasized about it before, and Roberto had been thrilled to hear they'd fulfilled a dream. (He'd been even more thrilled to hear that she'd masturbated to this particular fantasy.)

Anne had never really snuck around in high school—she didn't really date anyone seriously until she was in college, and her first time doing anything remotely sexual was when she was nineteen. So it was kind of fun to sneak around now. They were one movie trope away from him throwing rocks at her bedroom window.

Granted, they also spent a lot of time during the day working on the renovation—knocking things down and putting things up, painting and moving furniture and going over plans. But it was the kind of project Anne loved. She leaned back over her bullet journal page to add some embellishments.

Anne's phone buzzed. It was Roberto.

> ROBERTO: Hey wanna 'run an errand' with me to Silver Falls tomorrow?

Anne grinned and typed out a reply.

> ANNE: If by 'run an errand' you mean 'letting me ride you until you can't walk in Silver Falls' then yes.

ROBERTO: You read my mind.

ANNE: Do you actually have to go to Silver Falls tomorrow?

ROBERTO: Yes. But I was thinking about a certain hotel room that we once stayed together in without fucking, and I think we should revisit it.

ANNE: I think so, too.

Anne bit her lip to keep from grinning too widely.

THE NEXT DAY, AFTER "REVISITING" the hotel room thoroughly, Roberto laid on his back in the hotel bed and put his hands behind his head. Anne rested her head on his chest and smiled. She used one finger to lightly trace the tattoos on his shoulder, branches of a tree with vines curling around them.

"When did you get these?" she asked quietly.

Roberto took a moment to answer. "I started it when I was nineteen or so. I've added onto it over the years."

"I like it," Anne replied. It was sort of strange to imagine Roberto as a nineteen-year-old, sitting in a chair in a tattoo shop somewhere. It was a glimpse into what his life had been like for the past eight years.

After a few more minutes of silence, Anne spoke again. "What are you thinking about?" she asked.

"Honestly? About how much I wanted to fuck you the last time we were at this hotel."

Anne lifted her head and grinned at Roberto. "Really?"

Roberto nodded. "Really. I was like one second away from needing a cold shower that whole time."

"Wanna know the best and the worst part of this?" Anne said.

Roberto looked at her. "What?"

"I wanted to fuck you the last time we were at this hotel, too."

Roberto raised his eyebrows and smiled. "Yeah?"

Anne nodded. "Yeah. Although I don't know if I was quite as wound up. But there was a moment when I almost kissed you."

"I think I know what moment that was. When you were reaching for your phone?"

"Yep."

"Like this?" Roberto leaned over as if he was reaching for something on the nightstand.

Anne grabbed his face and pressed her lips to his. "Like that," she whispered.

CHAPTER 40

You've Got It Bad

ROBERTO

Roberto held Anne's hand as he drove them back from Silver Falls. Anne had declared herself too sleepy to drive and handed the keys to him. She was the one who had reached for his hand when they got in the car, and now that she'd fallen asleep with her hand in his, there was no way he could let go.

He glanced over at her sleeping form. Her red curls were pulled into two braids, and her makeup was still a little smudged from their time in the hotel room. He knew that when they got back to West Tindale, she'd flip the visor mirror down to fix it and then turn to him to ask if she looked okay. Roberto smiled at the thought.

He found he was enjoying the small, intimate little things of being with Anne for the last week and a half. Her asking him if she looked okay, her green eyes pure magic even when she was asking something so mundane. They'd risked spending the night together a few times, and he liked the way she kicked the blankets off her feet in the night. He liked her habit of biting her lip when she was thinking hard about something, showing off the gap between her teeth that she used to be so self-conscious about. He liked how she sometimes did a little celebratory dance when she got good news or something went well.

And there were things he'd forgotten about her, things that kept coming rushing back. They'd known each other so well for so long that he hadn't thought about some of these things in years. How she didn't like any of the food on her plate to touch. How the first thing she ate in the day had to be a breakfast food, no matter what time of day it was. And she still walked the same way as she had when they were seventeen—this purposeful stride, not wasting any time between points A and B.

Roberto wasn't sure if things would have been this good if they'd done this the summer they were seventeen. For one thing, they had been too young to know what they were doing in any sense of the phrase. And who knows, if they had done this that summer, they maybe never would have stopped. They'd probably be married by now, a car seat or two in the back, the kids sleeping as he drove them all home from Silver Falls.

The thought filled Roberto's chest with a glowing warmth. He still wasn't sure if he could be a husband and father, but suddenly, he could picture it so easily...the cabin he and Anne would share on the north side of town, or maybe one of the homes on Silverview Way. Bikes in the front yard. A high chair in the kitchen. Anne, reading in bed. A sense of longing filled him for a moment. But he pushed it all down.

It was just nostalgia, these thoughts. These were the daydreams he barely let himself have when he was young. It had been so long since he'd thought about any of these things that now they were just kind of taking up a lot of space in his head. It was only a fling, and then they could go back to their real lives.

Anne shifted slightly in her sleep, tightening her grip on his hand, and Roberto smiled.

Oh fuck, he thought. *I've got it bad.*

WHEN THEY GOT BACK to West Tindale (and after Anne had fixed her makeup in the visor mirror and turned to Roberto and asked if she looked okay), they sat in the driveway behind the bookstore and restaurant for a moment.

Anne smiled at Roberto. "I had a lot of fun today," she said. "And last night."

"You're just saying that because you came like, five times," Roberto replied.

Anne laughed. "That's definitely one of the reasons," she said. "Or five of them. But also I just like hanging out with you. I've liked the last week and a half."

"Same," Roberto said. He glanced around quickly to check that they were alone, then leaned forward and kissed her. He liked being able to just kiss her. When they came apart, she smiled at him.

"We should probably go inside," she said.

"Yeah," he replied, not breaking her gaze. "Although… do you mind if I borrow your car for a minute? I have another quick errand to run." He was still thinking about how big his feelings for Anne were getting, and needed a moment to get his head on straight.

"No problem," Annie said. "Just leave the keys downstairs when you're done." She smiled at him for another moment, then leaned in and kissed him passionately. She pulled back and held his gaze, a hint of a smile in her eyes. "Welp, see ya later!" she exclaimed, grinning. She opened the car door and walked away, not even looking back over her shoulder. She might have been swinging her hips a little bit for Roberto's benefit, but he couldn't quite tell. He leaned his head against the steering wheel.

"This is bad," he whispered, his stomach sinking. "This is real bad."

He ran upstairs and grabbed his running clothes, then got back into the car and headed into the park.

WHEN HE GOT to the Hughes Waterfall trailhead, he stepped out of the car. The Hughes Waterfall trail was mostly a boardwalk, and the wood made a steady rhythmic sound as he ran. He was halfway down the path when he realized it was where he and Anne and the rest of their friend group had gone stargazing after prom all those years ago. He jogged until he saw a bench and sat down. He pulled his phone from his pocket, then opened his notes app and re-read what he had written the first night in the hotel room in Silver Falls.

REASONS YOU SHOULD NOT KISS ANNE
WINSLOW
1. YOU ARE GOING BACK TO CHICAGO IN LIKE
A WEEK AND A HALF.
2. YOU HAVEN'T SPOKEN IN EIGHT YEARS.
3. YOU'RE NOT SURE IF YOU EVER WANT TO
GET MARRIED, AND SHE DOES WANT TO GET
MARRIED.
4. YOU DO NOT WANT TO LIVE IN WEST
TINDALE, AND SHE DOES.
5. YOU BARELY BECAME FRIENDS AGAIN,
MAYBE, SO DON'T FUCK IT UP.

He remembered how after he made the list that it really should have been "Reasons You Should Not Date Anne Winslow." The "not kissing" her part was long past. Roberto read through the list again. Reasons two and five weren't as relevant anymore. But the other three still were.

Roberto rubbed his hand over his face. He was really really enjoying this time with Anne, but he didn't want to make things even more difficult for himself when he had to leave. "It's just for now," he said out loud. He let the words move through him, shifting everything back into their rightful places. He stood up and started running back towards the car. "It's just for now."

CHAPTER 41
Wine and Insights

ANNE

When Anne got back up to her room after Roberto took the car, she closed the door behind her and fell onto her bed. She felt like a schoolgirl, giddy over a boy while she hugged her pillow. She glanced at the calendar on her wall.

Two weeks. Roberto was going back to Chicago in two weeks. It felt simultaneously so far away and like it was happening absurdly soon.

What was she going to do in two weeks? What would happen when he left? Would they text? Talk on the phone? Hook up when he was here for the holidays? But he'd never been here for the holidays. This was the first time he'd been back since he was seventeen. It was very possible that Anne would not see Roberto again for years.

It was possible that Anne would not see Roberto again, ever.

Anne buried her face in her pillow. She and Roberto had agreed to keep their fling quiet, but if ever a girl needed her best girlfriend, it was now. Anne weighed her options. She could either figure this out on her own, with no objectivity whatsoever, or tell the one person who already knew she'd slept with Roberto and hope she had a better perspective. Anne pulled out her phone and composed a text.

> ANNE: Hey, wanna come over tonight? I need your brilliant insights.

Maya replied right away.

> MAYA: See you at 8. I'll bring wine and crystals and tarot cards.

When Maya walked into Anne's room, she deposited Anne's car keys on the dresser. "Roberto just brought these by. I ran into him downstairs. Him and his stupid hot face."

"It is stupid hot," Anne replied with a grin.

"Wine?"

Maya poured out two glasses, handed one to Anne, and then the two of them sat cross-legged across from each other on the bed.

"Okay," Anne said. "Before I say anything, this is top secret. Like seriously, do not tell anyone, I am telling you in complete confidence, please please please keep it secret."

"Scout's honor," Maya said, holding up three fingers in the Boy Scout salute.

Anne took a moment, then spoke. "So the thing is that I didn't quite sleep with Roberto Bonino."

Maya looked at Anne in confusion. "So just, like… hand stuff, or…?"

Anne laughed. "No. It's more like…I'm…sleeping with Roberto Bonino?"

Maya grinned, set her wine glass on the nightstand, then fell backward and began flailing in a celebratory dance. "I fucking knew it!" she whisper-shouted. "I knew it! Fuck yes! This is so amazing!"

Anne couldn't stop smiling. "I know!" she whisper-shouted back.

"And I bet it's even better now that you've done it a few times. You need to have hot sex with him forever and then tell me about how hot it is forever."

"So the thing about that," Anne said, "is that he's going back to Chicago in two weeks and I don't really know what's going to happen after that and that's why I need your insight."

Maya was quiet for a moment while Anne waited. "Do you think you'll talk again after he moves away?"

"I don't know."

"Do you think you'll hook up again if he ever comes back?"

"I don't know."

"Do you want him to be your long-distance boyfriend?"

"I don't know."

Maya looked at the ceiling and then sighed. "Have you considered, and hear me out on this, have you considered talking to Roberto about this?"

Anne glared at her friend and set her wine glass down next to Maya's. "Well, when you put it that way…"

"I mean it," Maya said. "Just get on the same page. Tell him what you're thinking, how you're feeling." She looked at Anne for a moment. "How *do* you feel?"

Anne felt the weight of the question. She stared at her lap. "I don't…I don't know," she whispered. She thought for a few moments. "I know that the last week and a half is the happiest I can remember being in a long long time."

"You've been sleeping with Roberto for a *week and a half*?!"

"We wanted to keep it quiet!"

"Okay, fine, whatever, I love you, best friends forever. Okay, so you're the happiest you've ever been? And?"

"And…and that's all I know."

Maya nodded. "You want my actual insight?" she said.

"Yes, please."

"I think there are two questions here. One, and this is the big one, what are your exact feelings for Roberto Bonino? Like, on a scale of 'friends with benefits' to 'oh shit he's the love of my life,' where are you falling? Two, what are you going to do about whatever those feelings are?"

Anne felt a jolt run through her at the phrase "love of my life." But she smiled at Maya. "See, this is why I called you. I was too moonstruck to even get to those questions."

"Now you just have to figure out if you're twitterpated, or like…in love," Maya said.

Anne fell backwards onto the bed and stared at the ceiling. The size of that question seemed to fill every corner of the room. "Geez, Maya. 'In love,'" she said quietly. "Woof."

Maya crawled over and laid next to Anne. "Yeah."

One glass of wine and one tarot reading later, Maya left, and Anne thought about the question Maya had carried into the room. It was still there, floating in the air. Was she in love with Roberto Bonino?

What did "in love" even mean? How could she even tell? Was there an online quiz from *Psychology Today* or something? It seemed like something you just sort of knew. Like if you have to ask, you probably aren't?

When she tried to actually ask herself the question honestly, she felt like she was on the edge of a cliff. Like her toes were curled over the edge of something, and if she peered into the depths of her feelings for Roberto, she might find a well without end. And if he didn't swim in it with her, she might drown.

Anne thought about the times in her life when she felt she'd been "in love." There were probably varying degrees of it. The love she had felt for Tyler Young when she was a high school freshman was different from the love she felt for Garrett, and neither of those loves felt like what she felt for Roberto now.

The next day after work, Anne grabbed her keys and her journal and walked downstairs. Debbie looked up from the book she was reading.

"I'm going for a drive," Annie said. "Do you need anything?"

Debbie shook her head. "Have fun," she replied.

It was twilight as Anne drove into the park. She didn't have any particular destination in mind, but just driving through the park had always helped her clear her head. The trees and trails had a way of rearranging her insides to their rightful places. After Roberto had left, that summer before she went to New York, she had spent hours driving through Tindale Park. She'd do the Clark loop, driving in one big circle around the park, a full three hours. Sometimes she'd stop and walk somewhere, although for a long time she avoided the Hughes Waterfall boardwalk. Tonight, she pulled into the parking lot near it.

She turned on the car's interior light and opened her journal to where she'd pasted a single piece of paper in.

<u>Anne's Ideal Man</u>
(A revised list made at age twenty-five)
1. Appreciation for the arts. Doesn't necessarily have to be an artist, but someone who can enjoy museums and concerts and poetry with me.

2. Enjoys "the comforts of home." A fan of sitting in front of the fireplace or enjoying a meal with family or sitting in the backyard and chatting.
3. Willing to communicate. It sounds all trite and basic, but someone who's willing to say what's on their mind and ask questions and not be afraid of feelings.
4. Kind. Wants good things for the people he cares about. Compassionate.
5. Handsome.
6. Likes kids, or is at least interested in parenthood.

Anne sat back and looked out the window at the stars and trees of Tindale National Park. It was almost like a wave of something was coming barreling towards her, some realization she wasn't sure she was ready for. She closed her eyes and willed her breathing to slow down. She sat that way until she felt the waves subside.

Anne's phone buzzed. A text from Roberto.

> ROBERTO: Hey, can I put my hands and tongue all over your body tonight?

Anne couldn't help but grin. She may not have answers to the big questions, but she could answer this one.

> ANNE: Yes please.

An hour or so later, when Debbie had gone to bed, Anne heard Roberto's footsteps on the stairs. She'd left her door cracked, and he was smiling when he swung it open.

"You've got to learn to take your shoes off before you

come up here," Anne whispered from the bed, where she was lying with the blankets up to her chin.

"I like it when you take them off for me," Roberto whispered back. But he kicked them off anyway, then knelt at the foot of the bed and crawled towards her.

Anne pushed down the blankets down to reveal that she was already naked. "Sometimes there isn't time to take your clothes off for you," she said. Roberto looked down at her and grinned, then growled. His face was buried in her neck before she could say another word.

CHAPTER 42

Can I Try Something?

ROBERTO

Roberto still couldn't get over how good she felt. To feel her under his hands, to have their bodies pressed together, to be in the heat of her. Anne was bent over the edge of the bed, her hand working furiously between her legs. Roberto reached down and clutched her hips as he drove into her from behind, her small gasps and stifled moans almost sending him over the edge.

"I want...to...see you," she whispered, her words coming fast and desperate between gasps.

Roberto turned Anne over and wrapped his arms around her, laying her on her back in the bed. When he spread her legs and pushed into her again, her back arched. She bit her lip and looked into his eyes.

"Roberto, I'm..."

Roberto couldn't look away. He was crouched near the edge of the bed, her legs on either side of his ribs as he moved inside her, watching her face as she got closer and closer to orgasm. He reached a hand up and held the back of her head, holding her gaze. She never broke eye contact, even as her body tensed and her legs shook.

He came only seconds after she did. Afterwards, they both laid with their heads on the pillows, side by side.

After a few minutes, Anne turned to Roberto.

"I feel…naked," she said quietly.

"You *are* naked," Roberto replied.

"No, I mean…emotionally."

Roberto stared at the ceiling. If he thought about it, he felt the same way. What they had just done didn't feel like fucking. It had felt like making love. The thought made him feel strange and…alive.

"I um…" Roberto said. "I think I know what you mean." He turned his face to look at Anne. He could have sworn she was actually glowing. Was there a light on somewhere in this room that he hadn't noticed? Or was it actually just coming from Anne? He needed to change the subject, and fast.

"You touching yourself while I fuck you is the hottest thing on the planet," he said.

Anne smiled at him. "God, I'm glad you think so. I was with a guy once who literally told me not to. He said it was 'his job' to touch me to make me come or something dumb like that. I think he was trying to be hot, but he was also just really bad at touching me and didn't want any direction so I ended up just lying there and *not* coming."

Roberto was horrified. "That's terrible. What a stupid guy. Both because you didn't come and also because women touching themselves is hot as fuck."

"He was very stupid," Anne said.

Roberto put his hands behind his head and looked up at the ceiling, thinking about Anne's hand between her own legs and smiling. "I can't tell you how many times I've come just from watching women touch themselves. Of all the women I've slept with, it's consistently one of my biggest turn-ons."

Anne lifted her head and gazed at Roberto for a moment. "How many women?" she asked.

Roberto hadn't expected that question. "Uh…"

Anne raised her eyebrows. "Do you not know?"

Roberto was quiet. He didn't actually know…he hadn't kept track.

"Ballpark estimate," Anne said. "More or less than twenty?"

"More," Roberto said.

"More or less than thirty?"

He hesitated before answering. "Probably more."

"More than thirty?"

"I don't know. Probably?" Roberto felt suddenly self-conscious. "Well, how many people have you slept with?" he asked defensively.

Anne thought for a moment. "Nine…men," she finally said. "Including you. A few hook-up kind of things in college, and Garrett, when we were together, obviously. And a few tourists here in West Tindale."

Roberto had a moment of feeling intensely awkward, before something in Anne's statement caught his attention.

"Wait," he said, turning to her. "You paused before you said men. Have you slept with women?!"

Anne turned to him and smiled. "I've slept with one woman."

"Oh my god, that's so fucking hot," Roberto threw his head back and looked at the ceiling. "Was it hot? You don't have to tell me about it, but uh…you can tell me about it if you want to."

"You sound like a nineteen-year-old," Anne laughed.

"I don't care. I want you to tell me about the time you made it with a woman."

Anne shrugged. "Not much to tell. I was in college. We were at a party. It was enjoyable. I like women, but I'm pretty into men." She turned to him. "Have you ever done it with a man?"

Roberto shook his head. He'd had opportunities, but he could never quite feel enthusiastic about it enough to say yes.

"Threesome?" Anne asked.

Roberto paused for a moment, feeling awkward again, then nodded.

Anne was quiet, then said, "I know it's not a competition, but if it is, I'm clearly losing."

Roberto turned to her. "I'm just glad to be one of the people you've slept with," he whispered, caressing her face.

"Same," Anne said, smiling at him. She kissed him, long and slow and deep, then pulled away and looked into his face.

"Hey," Anne said. "Can I try something?"

"Sure," Roberto replied.

"Do you have it in you to go again?"

Roberto raised his eyebrows. "Just tell me what to do," he grinned.

"Stand up," Anne said.

Roberto threw off the blankets and stood beside the bed.

"Over there," Anne pointed to the middle of the room. She scooted to the foot of the bed and sat looking at him up and down. Her eyes rested on his cock, and just the way she was looking at him was making him hard again. Finally, she looked up into his eyes.

"I want you in my mouth," she said.

It definitely wasn't the first time a woman had said something like this to Roberto, but it had never made him feel this turned on this quickly.

"I...want to be in your mouth," he replied. He'd been thinking about it for...well, for a very long time. In the last week and a half, he'd spent plenty of time with his tongue between her legs, but she hadn't gone down on him. He figured they'd get around to it eventually. But now her lips on his cock were the only thing he could think about.

Anne lifted herself off the bed and knelt in front of him, taking his dick in her hands. He felt his blood rushing at her touch. She looked up at him, and Roberto couldn't think of anything more incredible than the sight. Her stunning eyes and her full lips and her incredible tits, all right down there in front of him.

"This isn't the first time I've done this," Anne said quietly. "But I think it's the first time I've *wanted* to do this."

"Wait. Really?" Roberto asked.

Anne nodded, stroking his cock slowly, still looking up at him. Roberto's cock twitched in her hand.

"I've done it because it was just part of what people do. Because men wanted me to. But it's always been because… because that. Because someone else wanted me to. With you, I want to. I want to taste you. I want to feel you in my mouth."

Roberto could only nod. Anne looked at his dick, then back up at him. "I don't know if I'm any good at this, so just…feel free to give me direction. If you want."

Roberto nodded again, and then Anne leaned forward and ran her tongue along the bottom of his shaft and he was suddenly weak in the knees. She was licking him up and down, agonizingly slowly. She swirled her tongue over the tip a few times, and when she finally closed her lips over the head of his dick and took his length into her mouth, Roberto's eyes rolled back into his head.

"God," Roberto whispered through gritted teeth. "Anne, this is…you're…"

Anne's lips were moving up and down his shaft, hot and wet and driving him insane. He reached down and rested one of his hands on the back of her head, not putting any pressure there, just steadying himself a little. She pulled back and his cock came out of her mouth with a pop.

She looked up at him and smiled. "This is as fun as I thought it would be," she said. "With you."

CHAPTER 43

The Truth is Here Now

ANNE

Anne was obsessed with how Roberto was looking at her. It was lust and desperation and vulnerability all at once. She kept her eyes locked on his face as she pulled him into her mouth again. She had been worried that she was bad at this, but Roberto seemed to appreciate what she was doing. He was watching her now with his jaw tight, whispering her name over and over. Anne had never felt sexier or more powerful in her life.

"Anne," Roberto whispered. "Anne, you're going to make me—"

Anne stood up and pushed Roberto backwards onto the bed, then laid beside him and pulled him over her.

"Not yet," she whispered. "I want to feel you inside me again." She reached up and moved her hands over her own breasts, looking into Roberto's eyes. He watched her face, then watched her hands, then leaned over to pull another condom out of the nightstand drawer. She loved the familiarity of it, somehow. Being naked underneath him, him knowing where the condoms were. His gaze never left her face when he pushed himself inside her, both of them moaning at the sensation. She reached down and drew circles over her clit with her fingers while Roberto began thrusting.

She couldn't believe how good it felt. It had never felt this good in her life.

As she felt the pleasure growing, Anne bit her lip and clung to Roberto's shoulders. She finally tightened around him, and he moved faster and more desperately until his body was tensing against hers. As she felt Roberto's orgasm pulsing through him, she clutched his body to her and spoke without thinking or planning it.

"I love you," she whispered. "I love you, Roberto. God, I love you."

As soon as she said it, she knew it was true. She'd probably known for a while. It seemed absurd to her that she'd ever even wondered. She'd known it the first time he had kissed her when they were seventeen, and she'd known it when she sat in the parking lot in Tindale National Park, reading over the list she'd made of her ideal man. It was the truth she had felt in the distance, but it was right here now.

When Roberto rolled off of her, they were both quiet. Anne's heart was pounding, both from her orgasm and from what she'd just said. She couldn't quite bring herself to look at Roberto. She could sense that he was staring at the ceiling, too.

"Roberto?" Anne whispered.

"Yeah?"

"I um…did you…hear what I said?" Roberto was quiet, and Anne finally turned her head to look at him when she spoke again. She took a deep breath. "I…I love you. I'm in love with you."

Roberto squeezed his eyes shut. It was almost like he was in pain. He was silent for a very very long time.

"It's just for now," he said. "We agreed that this was a fling, just for the few weeks that I'm here."

Anne almost heard an audible crack in her heart. She was having trouble breathing, like something was squeezing her chest so tightly, she might not survive it. She turned away from Roberto on the bed and curled into herself.

Roberto was quiet for another few minutes. Anne kept waiting, hoping that he'd turn towards her, curl his body around hers, press his lips to the side of her head and whisper "But I love you, too. I want to be with you."

After an agonizing silence, he just said, "I'm going to go."

Anne could only nod.

She lay there as she listened to Roberto get dressed, not looking at him. When he shut the door behind him, Anne allowed a tear to fall onto her pillow. Then she covered her mouth with her hand to stifle a sob. She stayed frozen like that until she heard Roberto's footsteps disappear all the way down the stairs, then pressed her pillow to her face and let the tears come. It was like her sadness was ripping through her, tearing her to shreds at a hundred miles per hour. It was an ache so deep she could feel it in the bones of her ribcage.

When the tears finally stopped, Anne dragged herself out of her bed and put on her pajamas. If everything was falling apart, maybe routine would help her tonight. She brushed her teeth and then sat down in her bed with her bullet journal, feeling shaky and exhausted.

She was staring blankly at the page when she heard a soft knock on her door. Her heart leaped with hope.

"Annie? Honey?" Her mother's soft voice came from the hallway. "Are you all right? Can I come in?"

Anne's heart crashed to the floor, and then she was

crying all over again. Within moments, Debbie had opened the bedroom door and come to sit on the edge of the bed. Without a word, she gathered Anne into her arms and just let her cry.

When Anne had finally cried herself out, she managed a hoarse whisper. "I'm in love with Roberto Bonino," she said.

"I know, sweetie. You have been for a long, long time."

Anne wasn't sure how to answer. She didn't know if her mom meant just in the last few weeks, or if these feelings had been there from the time she was young.

"I…I didn't know it. I didn't realize it until now, and now…" Anne had a hard time finishing her sentence.

"Have you told him?" Debbie whispered.

Anne nodded. "He doesn't…he says this was just a fling." A fresh wave of tears came.

"Oh, sweetheart." Debbie held Anne tighter, rocking her gently. Anne squeezed her eyes shut, clinging to her mother, feeling like a little kid again. She hadn't planned on telling Debbie about her and Roberto at all, but it seems like her mom already knew anyway.

"He's an idiot," Debbie finally said. "Just a dumb…idiot."

"He's not," Anne replied. "That's the worst part of it. If he was a dumb idiot, I could just let it all go, but he's wonderful and just doesn't want the same things I do."

"Are you sure he doesn't want the same things?"

Anne struggled to get her next sentence out. "He doesn't want me."

Debbie was quiet for a few moments. "Why don't you go to New York for a few days?" she finally said.

Anne lifted her head. "What?"

"You need to run away somewhere where you can heal your heart."

Anne was quiet as she looked at her mother. She seemed to be serious. Debbie gave her a small smile and added, "Sometimes you need to go to a place with different distractions to rearrange your soul."

"Mom, I can't afford to go to New York for a few days."

"Sure you can," Debbie said, smiling. "We've got $21,000."

"I can't use the donation money to just run away to New York," Anne replied.

"You can if you're shopping for wallpaper and decor and fabric for the new business. That's not running away. That's working on the renovation."

Anne thought for a moment, and Debbie kept talking. "I've been thinking about sending you to New York anyway, even before…before all this. We'll talk to Maya's parents about a deal on a hotel—maybe they can find a discount for you. You can stay in Manhattan for a few days, throw yourself into final design work, and not have to see Roberto or anything that reminds you of him for a little while."

Anne hugged her mother tightly and nodded.

CHAPTER 44
The Cemetery
ROBERTO

Roberto hardly slept. He lay in bed for hours, staring at the ceiling, a desperate weight on his chest. He'd done the right thing. There was no way his and Anne's lives could fit together, no matter how she felt. No matter how he felt. So why even try if it was impossible? It felt like shit to try.

If he were in Chicago, he'd call his guy and spend a huge amount of money on whatever party drugs were available and go on some kind of bender. He'd swipe on Tinder or go to a club. He'd do anything to get away from this feeling. Because this was not a pleasant feeling. But he wasn't in Chicago, so he just had to feel things.

He didn't see or talk to Anne at all over the next few days. He didn't text her, or call her, or go next door. He worked in his room.

A few mornings later, he stumbled into the tiny kitchen in the apartment above the restaurant. Cosimo was sitting at a small table, eating a bowl of cereal. Roberto collapsed into the other chair.

"Hey," Cosimo said.

"Hey," Roberto replied.

Cosimo studied him for a moment. "Is everything okay?" he finally asked.

Roberto leaned back in his chair, and then shook his head. Whatever was going on between him and Anne was definitely over now. And he didn't think he'd be able to hide how he felt about it.

"So uh," Roberto began. "I've kind of been sleeping with Anne."

"Oh, we know," Cosimo said.

"You *know*?" Roberto was tempted to punch him. He uncovered his face and looked at Cosimo.

"It's been pretty obvious, dude."

Roberto frowned. "Wait, you said 'we' know. Who's 'we'? Does everyone know?"

Cosimo nodded. Roberto laid his head on the table in defeat.

"Okay, well, yes, we've been sleeping together, and feelings have gotten involved and now everything is kind of terrible."

"Whose feelings?" Cosimo asked.

Roberto sat back up and paused. "The thing is that I live in Chicago and she lives in West Tindale so it's not going to work."

"That didn't answer my question. Whose feelings?"

Roberto didn't answer. Cosimo looked directly at him. "Are you uh…are you in love with Anne Winslow?" he asked.

Roberto paused. "I don't…I like her, definitely, a lot. Like, I care about her. But love is like, flowers and mixtapes and grand gestures," he replied.

Cosimo sat back in his chair. "I dunno, man, getting your company to match donations to save someone's family business seems like a pretty grand gesture. The kind of thing you do when you're in love with someone."

Roberto sat back in his chair as well. "Oh," he finally managed. All of his thoughts came to a screeching halt.

"Real talk?" Cosimo said.

"Do we have to?"

Cosimo smiled, then leaned forward. "Anne has been the love of your life since you were a kid, and you're still so caught up in the pain you felt when you were seventeen that you can't see it. You are so fucking afraid of losing someone again that you can't bring yourself to admit that you love them, even when they're right in front of you, offering you their whole heart. You've never actually faced losing mom and dad and now you can't embrace the love that's waiting for you in Anne."

There was a long silence. "Oh," Roberto finally said. Again. It was all he could think of to say.

"Come on," Cosimo said, standing up. "Come with me."

"Where are we going?" Roberto asked.

"Just grab your coat and come on."

Roberto sat in the passenger seat while Cosimo slowly drove them towards the south end of town. When they pulled into the cemetery, Roberto's fists clenched.

"What are we doing?" he asked.

"You're going to visit Mom and Dad's graves," Cosimo replied.

"I don't want to do that," Roberto said.

"I know you don't. And I'm not actually forcing you to. But I am dropping you off at their plot and not coming back for an hour. And you can either sit there at their graves and handle some of your shit or you can wander around until I come back."

Roberto glowered. Cosimo stopped the car and

pointed out the passenger side window at a spot twenty yards away. "There," he said. "That wide gray headstone, next to the tree." He leaned over further and opened Roberto's door. "See you in an hour."

"This is stupid," Roberto said. "I'm not going to do this."

"Then don't. But get out of my car."

Roberto let out an exasperated sigh and unbuckled his seat belt. "I forgot how annoying you are," he grumbled as he got out.

"Love you," Cosimo said, smiling. Roberto watched him drive away, then turned and looked towards his parents' graves.

When Roberto was younger, he loved this cemetery. It was filled with trees, and some of the headstones were hundreds of years old. He used to come here with Anne and Devan and Maya, just to walk around. When his parents had died, he'd left for Chicago within a week, and Cosimo had dealt with everything. Roberto hadn't even gone to the funeral. He didn't think he'd be able to stand it.

But maybe now, after eight years, he could try. He started walking, finally stopping in front of the headstone Cosimo had pointed to.

It was simple gray marble, with a heart between his parents' names. Tommaso and Gabriella. Roberto stood for a moment, trying to absorb the reality of it. His parents were *here*. They weren't at the restaurant, or in retirement somewhere, or back in Italy. They were here. An ache grew in his chest at the certainty of it. The finality of it. After a moment, Roberto sat cross-legged on the cold ground in front of the headstone.

"Hey," he said. He felt a little uncertain. He didn't know if this was what Cosimo meant by "handling some of his shit," but he wasn't sure how else to start. He glanced around the empty cemetery, then leaned forward slightly as he kept talking.

"Hi, Mom. Hi, Dad. It's uh…it's me. It's Roberto. I'm sorry it took me a while to get here. But um, I'm here now, so."

Roberto pulled his coat more tightly around him. It was mid-November, the days sliding towards winter, getting colder every day.

"I'm an architect now," he said. "In Chicago. I live in a big apartment. I um…I haven't been back here since… since I was seventeen. But I'm doing okay, now. I think."

Roberto looked at his parents' headstones again. He had eight years' worth of things to tell them. "I have some close friends in Chicago. My friends Lily and Kai are usually around. Lily and I used to date, but she's married to Kai now. And it's okay. More than okay."

Gazing at the headstone, Roberto noticed something beneath his parents' names that he hadn't noticed at first. Under the birth and death dates was a simple inscription. "Il mio amore per te attraversa gli oceani." *My love for you crosses oceans.*

Roberto thought of his parents, just lovesick teenagers in Italy, making plans. They'd only been seventeen when they'd eloped—the same age that Roberto and Anne had been when they'd first kissed. Roberto glanced up and looked over the cemetery.

There was no way he'd be able to pinpoint where they had laid in the grass, shoulder to shoulder at first, and then Roberto hovering over her. But he remembered how right it had felt. How when he'd pressed his lips to hers, it filled him up with something that felt like starlight.

And kissing her now felt that way, too. Images from the last month flooded him. Anne swinging the sledgehammer, covered in sweat, letting out a guttural yell. Anne leaning over her renovation notebook, pulling different colored pens out to make notes. Anne beneath him, the way she bit her lip when she came, her body convulsing around his. Her gap-toothed smile. Her red curls.

Roberto's parents had been willing to cross an ocean for each other. To leave everything they knew behind and step forward into the future, knowing that if they had each other, they'd be okay.

"What am I doing?" Roberto said out loud. His parents were willing to cross the entire Atlantic Ocean to be together, and he couldn't cross one time zone?

He had no idea how Anne's life and his life could fit together. He had no idea how any of it could work. But if his parents could trust the love they had for each other and figure out the logistics as they went, then maybe he and Anne could do the same thing. He knew that Anne knew what she wanted, and he knew what he wanted, and there was enough crossover that if they wanted each other, maybe they could figure out the rest. If the love was big enough.

Roberto laid his fingers on the headstone's inscription and closed his eyes. "I wish you were here," he whispered. "I wish you could talk me through this in person. I wish you could see how much Cosimo has done. I wish you could see who Anne is now. I miss you."

Roberto hung his head, and for the first time since he was seventeen, he cried for his parents.

Finally, he pulled out his phone.

"Hey Cosimo?" he said when his brother answered. "Can you come get me?"

CHAPTER 45

The Teacher

ANNE

Anne was packed and on her way to the Silver Falls airport by nine o'clock the next morning. Her eyes were puffy and red from crying, and she'd hardly slept. She'd given Maya an abbreviated version of what had happened between her and Roberto—just that she'd told him how she felt and that he didn't feel the same. Maya hadn't asked her any more questions when she'd come to pick Anne up, and now they were driving without talking, Maya humming to the radio occasionally. When they got to the airport, Maya hugged Anne fiercely.

"I love you," Maya whispered. "I can have Roberto killed if you'd like."

Anne managed a smile. "That's okay. I'll let you know if I change my mind."

Maya pulled away and held her friend at arm's length. "I'll do a spell of healing for you. Take this for now," Maya pressed a small satchel into Anne's hand. "Rose quartz for self-love, jet for holding sorrow. Go find your heart again," Maya said.

Anne hugged Maya once more, then turned and walked into the terminal.

Anne had booked a hotel for four days and three nights to start, with plans to stay longer if she needed. Anne spent the first day crying in her room before telling herself to get out into the goddamn city and "find her heart again," as Maya had said. Plus, she had things to do for the renovation.

She went to all of her favorite places from when she'd lived in Manhattan—the place in Chinatown that had the best dumplings she'd ever had in her life. The Drama Book-shop off of Times Square. She spent four hours in the Guggenheim on the second day, and then walked around in Central Park. She stopped in galleries and fabric shops along the way every day. She was surprised at how quickly the rhythm of all of it had come back to her. Swiping her Metro card, grabbing an egg and cheese bagel in the morning. It wasn't quite as overwhelming as she'd remembered. Or maybe she was just glad to have something to distract her.

She hadn't called or texted Roberto since he'd left her room that night. And he hadn't reached out to her. It was probably for the best, but it made her ache anyway.

On her final day in New York, she visited one last gallery. It was a small, independent group that always had rotating exhibits from NYU art students. It had been one of her favorite places to go when she was in college. She loved seeing everyone's work change throughout the school year. She wanted to find something for Pages and Pasta, something that would support some young artist. Anne was standing in front of an abstract painting of a moonscape when someone tapped her on the shoulder.

"Anne?"

Anne turned around and gasped. "Garrett?" she said.

It really was him, with a hint of early gray around his temples, his hair a little shorter now. His glasses were different, but it was him. It was disorienting to see him again, someone she'd loved and lived with and parted ways from.

She reached out to hug him. "Of all the gin joints in all the world," he said. He pulled away. "What are you doing here? I thought you were back in Missouri?"

"Montana," Anne said, smiling.

"Right, shit."

"I'm just here for a quick visit," Anne said. "I wanted to buy some art for the bookstore. We're renovating. How are you? What are you doing here?"

"I teach art at NYU, so I'm here with some students." Garrett gestured to a small cluster of people a few feet away, each of them looking at the art on display and writing in notebooks.

"You teach?" Anne said. "But you…uh, forgive me for saying this, but you always said you'd die before you became a teacher?"

Garrett laughed and shrugged. "It turns out that I actually really love teaching. I've been doing it for about two years now."

"Are you still painting, as well?" Anne asked.

"I actually just had a showing over at this place in Queens. I've been doing a lot more stuff with collage lately. I think you'd like it." Garrett paused. "What about you? Are you still…what are you up to?"

"I work for my family's bookstore back home. It's not as glamorous as New York, but I love it anyway. I'm really happy there." Anne allowed her eyes to roam over Garrett's face for a brief moment, before adding, "I still can't get over the idea of you teaching."

Garrett gazed at Anne for a moment, a warm smile on

his lips. "Sometimes you have to let go of plans in order for your life to fall into place," he said.

Anne smiled back. "I like that," she said. "I'm really happy for you."

"I'm happy for you, too," Garrett replied. He glanced over at his students. "I'm sorry, I've got to get back, but how long are you in town? I'd love to grab a cup of coffee and catch up?"

"I'm flying out later tonight," Anne said. "But it was good to see you. Truly."

They hugged again, and Anne watched him walk back to the group of students, thinking about how recently it seemed that she and Garrett were students themselves.

There was a time when watching Garrett walk away would have broken her heart into a million pieces. It had once. Even though she'd known it was the right thing, it had still felt like he was taking part of her with him.

She had mourned the future she'd imagined for them. They'd been living together for a year when he'd told her that he never wanted kids. She remembered standing in the kitchen, feeling the wind knocked out of her, astonished that they'd never had this conversation before. And then in little ways, for the next few months, she kept seeing the ways that they were walking in slightly different directions. If you start at a small enough angle of difference in your paths, it's not even noticeable at first. But eventually the distance is just too wide.

Anne watched Garrett out of the corner of her eye as she picked a painting and paid for it. She smiled and waved at him as she walked out the door. He raised his hand and smiled warmly.

In the cold outside, Anne thought as she walked towards the subway. *Sometimes you have to let go of plans in order for your life to fall into place,* he'd said. His words echoed in her head as she made her way back to the hotel. Anne pulled out her phone.

"Hello, love," Maya said when she answered.

"Have I been too attached to The Plan?" Anne asked.

Maya paused before answering. "I think you know how I'm going to answer that."

"I know you tease me about it," Anne said, "But I'm really asking. I'm wondering if…if maybe I've been too… closed off. Like, if maybe there are things I'm missing out on because they don't fit into some vision I have."

"You really want my opinion?" Maya said.

"Yes," Anne replied. "But give it to me kindly, please," she added.

"I think your plan is beautiful. I think it's beautiful that you know what you want, and that you guard that vision fiercely. There's something really powerful in that."

"But?" Anne said.

"But. I think there's still room within that plan for some, I dunno, flexibility. Like, it's not that your plan is too rigid, exactly. But sometimes it seems too small. Like, it could be expanded to include even more than what you've envisioned."

Anne felt Maya's words balloon in her chest.

"Are you saying I could envision even more for myself?"

"Yes."

Anne thought for a moment. "But how do I know if I…deserve it?"

"Deserve it? Anne, no one deserves anything! And everyone deserves everything! If it comes to you, you can have it! I know that sounds all witchy but I'm a witch and I think Roberto's in love with you and you guys could make it work if you wanted it to. It would at least be worth it to try."

Anne's eyes filled with tears. She was so tired of crying. "I don't know if he is. I don't think he is. When I told him, he didn't…he wasn't…"

"Anne," Maya said. "Roberto Bonino has been in love with you since you were both fourteen years old. I think you both just need to trust that."

CHAPTER 46

Crossing Time Zones

ROBERTO

"Hi, Debbie," Roberto said as he rushed through the bookstore and started up the stairs to the Winslow family's apartment. She was sitting on a stool behind the counter, a book in her hand.

"Anne? Anne!" Roberto called her name as he took the steps up to her room two at a time.

"She's not here," Debbie called out.

Roberto had just raised his fist to knock on Anne's door. He came back down. "Where is she?" Roberto asked.

"She's in New York," Debbie said.

Roberto blinked. "I need to talk to her. When will she be back?"

"I'm not sure," Debbie said. "She wasn't sure how long she needed."

"How long she needed for what?"

Debbie looked at him very closely. "You know for what, Roberto." Roberto stared at the ground, his stomach dropping. He had an ache in his chest so deep he didn't think anything but holding Anne would soothe it.

"She's also getting things for Pages and Pasta," Debbie added.

Roberto nodded, then turned around and jogged back to the restaurant side of the building. There were a few patrons sitting in booths, and Cosimo was in the kitchen. "She's in New York," Roberto said.

Cosimo looked at him. "You could…call her?"

"This doesn't feel like a phone call kind of conversation," Roberto replied. "It would be like breaking up with someone over text. But like, the opposite. But even besides that, Debbie doesn't know when she'll be back. She's there indefinitely, and I don't know how long I can wait." Roberto leaned on the counter and thought for a moment, then looked up at his brother. "Should I go to New York?"

"Is it a crossing time zones kind of love?" Cosimo asked. Roberto smiled. "I'll close up early and drive you to the airport."

Roberto had an entire flight to think about what to say to Anne, and how to say it. He had a decent rough draft in his head by the end of the flight, and a long note in his phone. But when he landed at JFK, it occurred to him that he didn't actually know where Anne was staying. Somehow he'd only thought as far as telling her how he felt. The rest of the details were hazy. It was a grand romantic gesture with very little thought about the logistics.

He stood in the middle of the airport, with just his wallet, his phone, and his keys, wondering what to do next. It occurred to him that if Anne were here, she would know what to do next. She'd have a plan. She'd have a whole bullet journal full of detailed plans. The thought made

Roberto's heart swell. Finally, he pulled out his phone to call Debbie and ask her about where Anne was staying, but the next thing he realized was that he didn't have Debbie's number. So he called Cosimo instead.

"I need to know where Anne's staying," Roberto said into the phone.

"Robbie, you did not plan this well."

"Yes. I know. But if you could just text me Debbie's number, I can ask her where—"

"No, I mean like you really did not plan this well. Anne's on her way back here."

Roberto froze.

"You mean she's not in New York?"

"She still might be, but she's coming back to West Tindale today. Right now."

Roberto looked around. "Is she flying out of JFK?"

"I don't know, hold on." Cosimo put the phone down and yelled something to someone in another room, then got back on the line. "LaGuardia," he said.

"Dammit. Okay, lemme see if I can catch a flight back to Silver Falls. Can someone come get me if I make it back tonight?"

"We've got you," Cosimo said. "Just keep us posted."

"Thank you," Roberto said. "Hey."

"Yeah?"

"I, uh…I love you. I know I haven't said it much, but uh…yeah."

Cosimo paused, and Roberto could hear the smile in his voice when he replied. "You're making all kinds of grand gestures today, man. I love you, too."

Roberto spent the next twenty minutes on his phone, trying to find a flight back to Montana, with zero luck. Another twenty minutes at various ticket counters had the same result. The soonest he could get back to Silver Falls was going to be tomorrow afternoon.

Roberto collapsed into a chair and hung his head in his hands. His phone rang. As soon as he saw the name on the screen, he picked it up.

"Anne!" he said.

"Roberto? My mom just texted me to tell me that you're in New York? What are you doing here?"

"I need to talk to you. Are you still at LaGuardia?"

"I'm sitting on the plane—we're about to take off. What do you need to talk about?"

"Oh my god. Um. I—"

"Can it wait? The flight attendant is glaring at me to put the phone away."

"Anne, I need to talk to you in person, but I can't get a flight to Silver Falls until tomorrow afternoon. Do you…I don't…"

"I have a layover in Chicago," Anne said.

Roberto blinked.

"Chicago O'Hare Airport," Anne said. "It's halfway between New York and Silver Falls."

"I'll meet you there," Roberto replied.

Roberto found a flight to Chicago O'Hare that was boarding within the hour. He paced in front of the gate, and had a hard time sitting still once he was seated on the plane. He glanced at his phone. 6 p.m. Between the flight time and the time zone change, it would be close to 8:30 p.m by the time he landed. Anne would have to wait at the airport for an hour. He hadn't told her where to meet him, but now her phone was off.

Maybe this was a terrible idea. *I really should have planned better,* he thought. Who wants to talk about their feelings in an airport, during a layover?

It was surreal to think that he'd been in West Tindale just this morning. Was it really just this morning that he stood at his parents' graves? He shook his head. At least he had plenty of time before he saw Anne to make sure he knew what he wanted to say.

CHAPTER 47
Starlight
ANNE

When Anne landed at Chicago O'Hare, she turned her phone on the second she was allowed to. A text from Roberto chimed.

> ROBERTO: Let me know what gate you're at and I'll come to you.

When she stepped out into the airport, she looked up and sent her reply.

> ANNE: B9

And then there was nothing to do but wait. She rolled her suitcase over to a chair and sat down. Then stood up again. Then sat down again. Somewhere deep in her center, something she hardly dared to name was fluttering, a tiny little song of hope. But maybe he just wanted to apologize in person, or explain. Or something.

If Anne smoked, she would have sat in the smoking lounge and gone through two packs of cigarettes. Instead, she attempted to distract herself with games on her phone (which didn't work) and trips to the bathroom to fix her hair and makeup (which also didn't work). She kept glancing at the time. He should be here in fifteen minutes. Anne began pacing. Ten minutes. Seven minutes. She sat and watched the hallway. And when she turned to look down the other direction, she froze.

She saw Roberto a moment before he saw her. He was wearing jeans and a light blue button-up shirt, and the color showed how stunningly blue his eyes were, even from far away. His dark hair was messy around his face, and Anne was sure that she had never loved anyone more in her life.

Roberto caught her eye, and his face was unreadable. She slowly stood and walked to meet him.

"Roberto," she said. She couldn't think of anything else to say.

He gazed at her. "I couldn't find a flight to Silver Falls and I couldn't stand waiting one more minute than I had to. I need to tell you. I…"

Roberto looked into her face and paused. Anne felt like her heart was going to explode, whether from love or heartbreak, she couldn't tell. She placed on hand on her chest to steady her breathing.

"Hang on," Roberto said. "I made a list."

Anne couldn't help smiling, even if she was still unsure what he was going to say. "You made a list? Roberto Bonino made a list?"

"I made this list that first night in the hotel room. In Silver Falls. I told myself I shouldn't kiss you, or date you, and I made a list to remind me why."

Anne frowned. She wasn't sure what she was expecting, but it wasn't this. "You…you wanted to meet me in a

Chicago airport to tell me why you shouldn't kiss or date me?"

Roberto looked at her. "I know how this sounds, but I just…stick with me for just a minute."

Anne waited and Roberto spoke while he searched his pockets for something, still talking.

"I told myself that I couldn't be with you because you wanted to stay in West Tindale and I live in Chicago, and because we hadn't spoken in years, and because we barely became friends again and I didn't want to fuck it up." Roberto stopped and looked up at her. "But I…what I feel for you…Anne, I'd cross time zones for you."

Anne's heart thumped in her chest. "You'd what?" she asked.

"I'd cross time zones for you. My parents crossed an ocean for each other, and I'd do that for you."

Roberto was looking at her with so much sincerity, and Anne couldn't quite find words for how it made her feel. Roberto took a step closer and took Anne's hands in his.

"I love you," he whispered. "I'm in love with you, Anne Winslow. I always have been."

Anne closed her eyes and smiled. She held back tears as she whispered, "I feel like I'm filled with starlight."

Roberto smiled at her. "That's how I feel when I'm around you."

They stood like that for a moment, facing one another. Then Roberto shook his head. "Dammit. Anne, I love you. But—ugh, I had a plan! I was going to read you the one list first, and then read you the other, more important list, and that was going to be the part where I told you I'm in love with you."

Anne laughed. "You had *two* lists?"

"Hang on. Listen," Roberto pulled out his phone and read from it.

"Reasons Why I'm In Love With Anne Winslow: One, Anne sees beauty in everything around her. In people, in books, in Tindale National Park. Two, she speaks in poetry. Three, she's hot as fuck." Anne laughed. "Four, she makes me see a future for myself that I thought I had to give up. Five, when I'm with her, I feel like my best self. My truest self."

"I feel like I'm my truest self with you, too," Anne replied. Roberto put his phone back in his pocket, then lifted Anne's face to his, and pressed his lips to hers. The song of hope that had been fluttering inside of Anne burst into a full orchestra of joy. She was surprised her feet were still planted on the floor. She was sure her happiness was big enough to lift her right into the air. When they finally pulled apart, Roberto rested his forehead against Anne's, cradling her face in his hands.

"Come home with me," Roberto said softly. "Just for tonight. We'll figure the rest out later. Tonight, just be with me."

They took a Lyft to Roberto's apartment. In his dim bedroom, they undressed slowly and made love slowly, moving together in rhythm. *I get to have this,* Anne thought as she ran her hands over Roberto's body. The remarkable happiness of it was startling, every time she thought of it. Afterwards, Anne fell asleep with her head on Roberto's chest, feeling his lungs rise and fall.

When Anne woke, she heard the shower running. She glanced at her phone. 9 a.m. She laid back and smiled to herself as she looked around the room. Roberto's apartment was simple, but there was lots of art on the walls. An entire life that he'd built away from her. But whatever his life was, she would get to be a part of it now.

"Good morning," a low voice rumbled. Anne glanced up to find Roberto, dripping from the shower, a towel wrapped around his waist. Anne followed a water droplet from his neck, down his chest and stomach and into the towel. When she looked back up at Roberto's face, he was smiling at her, eyebrows raised.

"I just…I can't believe I get to have you," Anne finally managed.

Roberto pulled the towel off with one hand and walked towards the bed. Anne's eyes strayed down between his legs as he knelt on the edge and cupped her face in his hands. "I can't believe I get to have *you*," he whispered. He kissed her softly, and Anne melted into him. Afterward, she kept her eyes closed for a long moment.

"Roberto, when you left…when we were seventeen…"

Roberto sat beside her on the bed. "I'm so sorry, Anne. I don't have any excuse besides the fact that I was seventeen and scared out of my mind, and so heartbroken I couldn't think straight. I felt like…I felt like I was made out of glass, and that when I shattered, I cut everyone around me, so I had to just run away for a while. I didn't want to cut you." Roberto studied Anne's face.

"Leaving cut me," Anne said quietly.

"I know." Roberto paused for a long moment, years' worth of pain and sorrow in his eyes.

"I loved you, even then," he finally said.

"I loved you, too," Anne replied. She leaned in and kissed him.

After what was either five minutes or fifty, Roberto pulled away. "I um…I don't…we should probably figure out…"

Anne smiled. "Are you trying to tell me that you didn't plan beyond your beautiful confession of love?"

"I am telling you that."

"So would now be a good time to tell you that I have an idea for a plan?"

Roberto smiled. "I love you, Annabelle Winslow," he said. He took her hands in his. "I'm glad there was room in your plan for me."

"I love you, Roberto Bonino. I'm glad you made it into my plan after all."

Epilogue

TWO YEARS LATER

Anne pulled a chair out from the table at Pages and Pasta to accommodate her enormous belly. The baby kicked as she lowered herself into the seat. She laid a hand over her stomach. "Calm down, Tommaso," she said quietly. She'd been joking that he would be either a track star or a dancer, with how much he moved.

She heard the sound of the door open. Anne called over her shoulder. "We're closed."

"It's me!" Roberto's voice replied. "I brought you and baby the carrot cake you asked for."

"Oh, bless you," Anne said. Roberto leaned down to kiss her lips, then set a box down on the table in front of her.

"Annie! Guess what just showed up? The fabric for the tablecloths!" Debbie's voice echoed from the back room.

"Oh, thank god!" Anne started to get up, but immediately changed her mind. "Yeah, I'm way too pregnant to get out of this chair right now." She raised her voice to call back to her mother. "Can you bring them in here?"

Debbie exited the back room with armfuls of different

colored gingham. "Good lord, you're more pregnant every day," she said, setting the fabric down on the table.

"You're telling me," Anne replied. She started sorting through the fabric. "These are perfect," she said.

"And just in time, too," Debbie said.

"Fabric in time for the wedding, and a wedding in time for the baby," Roberto added.

"I know most people don't get married when they're eight and a half months pregnant," Anne said, "But I guess our timing has always been our own."

"I don't know, my timing always seems to satisfy you," Roberto replied with a wink. Anne grinned at him.

"If *either* of you had any real sense of timing," Debbie said, "You'd have had this baby in the spring, when you're normally in West Tindale, and not in the fall, when you're normally heading back to Chicago."

"We didn't do it on purpose, Mom," Anne said. She glanced at Roberto. She was a little worried about his job. It had been hard enough to convince Jiménez Building Design to let him live in West Tindale for six months out of the year.

But when Anne and Roberto had gotten together, it had seemed like the best compromise they could come up with. And it worked. They spent April through September in West Tindale, helping Debbie and Cosimo with Pages and Pasta during the busy tourist season and staying in a tiny apartment a few blocks from the KOA. Then October through March, they stayed in Chicago while Roberto worked as an architect, saving money to help them make ends meet during the months they were away. But with the baby due in October, they'd decided to stay in West Tindale for the winter. They'd moved into their new place a few weeks earlier.

"I'm actually looking forward to staying in West

Tindale for the year," Roberto said, rubbing Anne's shoulders. "I'm planning on honing my manly Western instincts up at the cabin. Chop wood. Repair fences."

"Change diapers," Anne finished for him. She grabbed his hand and placed it on her belly. The baby kicked under Roberto's hand. He knelt beside her and kissed her belly.

"I brought the flowers!" a voice rang out. Maya walked in through the front door. Or at least Anne assumed it was Maya, since it was Maya's voice. Maya herself was completely hidden behind several enormous bouquets.

"Put them over here," Debbie said.

Maya made her way over to the counter, where Debbie was making room. "There," Maya said. She looked at her best friend. "You are so fucking pregnant."

"I know," Anne replied.

"Language, Maya," Cosimo said, walking in from the café's kitchen. "The baby can hear you!"

She rolled her eyes at him. "The first thing I'm gonna do as a godmother is teach this baby how to cuss," Maya said.

Anne laughed. "I'm so excited for you to be a godmother."

"I haven't been this excited for you since the night we all forced you and Roberto to share a hotel room in Silver Falls," Maya replied.

"Since the night you *what*?!" Anne yelled.

"Oh. Oops," Maya said.

Anne looked at Cosimo and her mom. "Did you all force Roberto and I to share a hotel room in Silver Falls?!"

Cosimo grinned, and Debbie pretended she couldn't hear the conversation.

"Oh, we definitely got your messages that night," Maya said. "I just convinced everyone to ignore you so that you'd be thrown together like in a cheesy rom com."

"I can't believe you did that," Roberto said.

"Well," Maya replied. "It worked, didn't it?"

Roberto and Anne smiled at each other. "I guess it did," Roberto said.

"Eventually," Anne added.

She glanced around, flowers and fabric and signs laid out all over. She'd kept careful track of everything in a notebook, but now there wasn't much more to be done. Tomorrow afternoon, they would bring some of the flowers to Tomasso and Gabriella's graves. Anne's mother would help her finish the table decorations for the wedding. Anne would put a flower crown in her hair, and then she would stand across from Roberto in the doorway between what used to be the bookstore and what used to be the restaurant…the place where they had knocked down a wall two years ago. They'd exchange rings and promises, surrounded by the people who had loved them both from the very beginning. It wasn't the Tindale Lodge wedding Anne had envisioned when she was fourteen, but sometimes you've got to let go of a few things in order for the rest of your life to fall into place.

She couldn't think of a better plan.

Halfway Across The Street

EXCERPT

Another roll of thunder passed overhead, this one a little louder. Maya glanced over her shoulder toward town, and when she felt the first drop of rain, she decided to head back. And it was a good thing, too, because in a matter of minutes, it was pouring, and Maya was soaked through. She held her forearm over her eyes to try and shield them from the rain, but it was already almost impossible to see.

"Goddammit," she said, trying to keep her eye on the path below her feet. The ground was soon becoming too muddy to walk easily, and the path was quickly disappearing. There was really no way to tell which direction she was going. She stopped and tried to look up to see if there were any large trees nearby where she could take shelter until the worst of the storm had passed, but she kept having to swipe her hair out of her eyes. She couldn't remember if she'd ever seen it rain this hard.

Maya stood and thought. The storm couldn't last forever, and she probably wouldn't actually die if she had to stay in it for a little while. And she could try to follow the path, but the chances of her losing it and wandering into the park were higher than normal. She was standing and trying to decide what to do, when she was startled by a hand on her shoulder.

Maya jumped and screamed, and was about to start swinging when she recognized the tall figure in front of her.

"Tanner?" she said. She practically had to yell to be heard over the storm.

"Come on!" he said. "There's a tree over here!"

He held out his hand. Maya hesitated, and then she took it. Tanner led them a few yards off the path to a large pine, its branches thick and spread wide, creating a small circle of protection close to its trunk. Maya bent over, squeezing the water out of her hair. When she stood back up, Tanner was standing a few feet away and looking at her with an expression she couldn't quite read. His brown curls were wet, and water dripped down his face. Maya's eyes roamed over the drops near his temples, at the hollow of his throat.

"What are you doing out here?" she finally asked. Here in the shelter of the pine, the rain was muted slightly.

"I could ask you the same question," Tanner said.

"I was going on a walk."

"So was I."

The two of them looked at one another for a moment. Then Maya glanced out at the rain, still coming down in sheets. She sank down to the dry(ish) ground and sat with her back leaned against the trunk of the tree. After a moment, Tanner joined her. She was suddenly aware of the heat of his body, close next to her.

"Thanks," Maya said. "By the way. I guess."

"No problem," Tanner said.

Maya glanced at him. He was running a hand through his hair, shaking the water out of it. His hazel eyes were gazing out at the rain.

"I'm not a damsel in distress," she said.

Tanner looked over at her. Maya had to stop her breath from catching. She hadn't realized how close they were sitting.

"I didn't need rescuing," she managed to continue. "But I'm glad you…but I…thank you."

Tanner nodded, then turned his face back towards the park. He leaned his head back against the trunk of the tree. "I know you're not a damsel in distress, but I do keep rescuing you, don't I?"

Maya frowned. "When else have you rescued me?"

Tanner turned to her, searching her face for a moment. "That night at the bar. When that drunk guy wouldn't leave you alone."

Maya was stunned. Her frown deepened, and she felt anger flood her chest. "Oh, was that what you did?" she said. "You stick up for some fellow asshole misogynist who wouldn't leave me alone, then glare at me like I wouldn't give this poor guy a chance? You call that 'rescuing me'?"

Tanner's face mirrored Maya's frown. "I was…" he started. Maya watched him turn away and swallow hard.

"I didn't mean to glare at you," he said.

Maya felt her irritation deepen. "Then what do you call what you did?"

Tanner drew his knees up a little and rested his forearms on them. She watched as he traced a long scar on the side of one hand. "Engaging the aggressor," he said quietly.

"What?"

"I don't know what it's actually called, but I just…I know that sometimes when women reject men, they can get…violent. Or dangerous. The men can, I mean. And they do the same thing when someone confronts them about what they're doing. So if you can sort of…distract the aggressor, it's easier to keep everything calm. I didn't want anyone to get hurt, so I just started talking to the guy to give you a chance to get out of there. If you needed it."

For a long time, Maya couldn't think of anything to say. Finally, she asked, "Why did you glare at me afterwards?"

Tanner shook his head. "I didn't mean to. I was trying to check in with you, make sure you were okay. Maybe my face just looks more glare-y than I realized."

Maya leaned her head back against the tree. She thought back to that night at the bar. Tanner's method had worked. She had been able to escape the drunk creep who wouldn't leave her alone, and no one had gotten violent or threatening.

"Why didn't you just punch the guy?" Maya asked.

Tanner looked at her and she saw something pass over his face. "I wanted to," he said quietly. "I just thought the other method would work better in the long run."

"You should tell people that that's what you're doing," she said.

He smiled at her, and the sight of it filled Maya's blood with what felt like champagne fizz. His teeth were white and straight, but it was the way his eyes crinkled, the way his whole face changed when he smiled. It caught Maya off-guard, and she couldn't quite think for a moment.

"It doesn't work as well if you tell people what you're doing," he said.

They stayed like that for a moment, sitting side by side, looking at each other, Tanner's smile warm and open, Maya's heart speeding up.

A clap of thunder startled them both out of their shared look.

"Good lord," Maya said, peering out at the storm. The rain wasn't coming down any harder, but the thunder definitely sounded closer.

"I really hope the roof of the old schoolhouse doesn't leak," Tanner said. Then he glanced over at Maya. "Sorry," he said. "That was…sorry."

Maya felt everything in her deflate. "I hope the roof does leak," she said. She meant to sound snarky, but it came out more petulant than anything.

Tanner glanced over at her. "I'm sorry. About the old schoolhouse. It's just…it's important to me."

Maya got up and then sat directly across from Tanner.

"Why?" she said.

"Why what?"

"Why is it important to you? Tell me."

~

Halfway Across the Street

Available on Kindle Unlimited, Amazon, Bookshop.org, and on order through your favorite local indie bookstore

September 2025

Acknowledgments

Special thanks to Andy, Brittany, Mikah, and Katrina for being the best beta readers ever. (Andy, thank you for punching my babies, and Mikah, thank you for helping me be anti-racist and also for being my ride-or-die in general.) Thank you, Brittany, for your very smart notes, and thank you Katrina, for your empowering encouragement.) Thanks to Aaron Woodall for assisting with the Italian. Huge thanks to Chloe (@ctinneyart on Instagram) for her incredible artwork for the cover art of the first publication of this book, and massive thanks to Sam Palencia at Ink & Laurel (@Inkandlaural on Instagram) for her cover art on the new edition.

Some special love to my "Fridays at Two" girls, Bran, Darcy, and Carrie—your friendship continues to sustain me through every one of my moonstruck endeavors, and I feel so lucky that I get to hurtle through space on this rock with you.

I also owe an enormous debt to Ava Munroe for her invaluable guidance in self-publishing—this would have been so much more difficult without your resources and recommendations. Additional shout outs to David Gaughran's free courses on self-publishing and book marketing, and the 20BooksTo50K Facebook group. Thanks to IHOP and Sugarhouse Coffee for being my favorite writing places, and to NaNoWriMo for giving me the scaffolding and motivation to start writing novels years ago.

And finally, thank you to my mom, for always taking me to the library as a kid, even if I sometimes snuck off to read a few pages from the "grown-up books" (the ones with half-naked people on the covers).

Also by Elle Whittaker

WEST TINDALE

Halfway Across the Street (September 2025)

Halfway Through the Holidays

ROCK ROMANCE

Rules Worth Breaking (July 2025)

Kisses Worth Waiting For (October 2025)

ENCOUNTERS

Under His Hands

At Your Service

OTHER THINGS

Jane Eyre and Zombies

About the Author

Elle Whittaker is the pen name for Liz Whittaker, who is the daughter of a poem and an ancient Egyptian hieroglyph. She spent most of her time on the shores of Neverland before moving to Salt Lake City, where she currently lives in a library until she can afford an RV. Her heart alternates between pumping lemonade and ink. Her favorite foods are music and knowledge, which she eats as often as possible from atop her mountain of crippling student debt. Her other job is theatre. In her free time, she enjoys hugging trees, completing jigsaw puzzles, and thinking about outer space. She is happily a victim of the kind of moonstruck madness that drives her to not only write romance novels, but poetry, scripts, essays, and theatre reviews under various names.

instagram.com/ellewhittakerromance

tiktok.com/@elle.whittaker.romance